DARKNESS

in the

LIGHT

J. K. Lincoln

Ralston Store Publishing
P.O. Box 1684
Prescott, Arizona 86302

ISBN 978-1-938322-44-0

Professionally edited by:
Jennifer Hope
www.MesaVerdeMediaServices.com

Printed in the USA.

"Hope is being able to see that there is light
despite all of the darkness."
~~Desmond Tutu

PROLOGUE

THE DOORBELL RANG, and Olivia Vandermeer involuntarily looked at the clock. She didn't know why she always did that, but maybe because she knew she wasn't expecting anyone. Standing up and walking toward the front door, she hesitated at the mirror and smoothed down her hair as she checked to see if her makeup looked all right. It did.

Before Olivia could reach the door, the doorbell was followed by a knock. When she opened it, she found the postman walking away from a package that he had left on her doorstep. He turned when he heard the door. "Miss Vandermeer, I knew you'd want to know when this arrived!"

"Thank you!" she called after him, as she smiled and bent to pick up the package. Amazon. Her book had arrived! Olivia couldn't wait to open it and begin reading it. Again.

CHAPTER ONE

OLIVIA THOUGHT SHE should call Dean and tell him the book arrived, but he wasn't off work for several more hours. Besides, she could barely wait to start reading it—even though she'd already read it a dozen times—*and* had written it. Sinking down into her recliner by the front window, she opened the box and held the book up in front of her, smiling the whole time. *There's a Darkness in the Light* by Olivia Vandermeer. Then she quickly checked the formatting of the book and began reading.

Never Run Out of Gas in a Place Like This

THAT WEDNESDAY STARTED benevolently enough. Holly left at dark-thirty so she could arrive at her destination while it was still light. Her old, blue Toyota Tercel was fueled, and she had a to-go thermos of her good, stout coffee. It would keep her awake for the long drive ahead of her. But falling asleep at the wheel would probably have been preferable to the horror that awaited her.

She had taken a week and a half vacation time from her job as manager of a travel agency. Although she could have flown for free, she preferred traveling alone in her car. Some of her friends thought it might make her feel lonely. But it didn't—it made her feel free. And she loved the feeling of that kind of freedom.

Combing her long, blonde hair as her car raced down the interstate, she glanced quickly in the rearview mirror to make sure her part was straight. It made her remember her early high school days when she would apply her makeup on the way to school: mascara, eye shadow, and eye liner that all highlighted her sky blue eyes. It was a miracle she didn't put an eye out or have an accident doing all that while driving. But she couldn't do it at home.

Her mother had said that Holly was beautiful without makeup and that the only reason she wore it was because of peer pressure. In her heart, Holly had known that her mother was right, but since everyone else used makeup, she felt that she had to also. After her mother was killed, she stopped wearing makeup altogether. Traffic at a busy interchange brought her back from thoughts of the past.

The road stretched out long and flat before her, and she smiled as she thought how wonderful it was going to be to surprise her friend Becky. It was a twelve-hour drive to the little town outside Oklahoma City where Becky had just moved, and the poor girl still didn't know anyone in town.

2

Becky was still unpacking, and Holly wanted to help. So she had taken the time off, and here she was, driving on I-40, listening to the radio, and thinking about Route 66.

Although it was no longer intact, that highway had meant a lot to Holly's grandparents, because they had driven the whole of it on their honeymoon. Her grandparents had raised her after her parents died in a car crash, and now her grandparents were gone too. She was alone in the world, but Becky was her best friend, and Holly could hardly wait to surprise her.

She had just crossed the Texas border when she realized she needed gas. Desperately. But she passed by the tiny ghost town of Boise which wouldn't have a gas station anyway. A few miles farther when the needle slipped past empty on her gas gauge, she realized that she couldn't make it all the way to Adrian. Frantically, she began searching the desolate landscape for something that might resemble a town. Holly had thought there was farmland in Texas, but there wasn't much of it on this lonely stretch of highway. Finally, she saw an offramp for Plenty, Texas. She didn't have a choice. The final-one-gallon indicator had already come on. So she hoped they had *plenty* of gas.

Several miles passed—while she held her breath waiting for the car to sputter to a stop—before she saw the town. Luckily, they had a gas station. It would probably be outrageously expensive, but at least she would have gas. She thought she was probably driving on fumes when her car glided in next to a pump. The station was a small place, with only two pumps and a tiny convenience store, but they had gas and they had restrooms, and right then, that was all that mattered. The only other car on the premises was a raggedy sheriff's car, parked in front.

Reaching over for her leather purse on the passenger seat, she pulled out her credit card and stepped out of the car. Looking at the pump, she laughed. Although the building behind her looked almost new, the pump looked ancient. It was difficult to see the numbers behind the dirty glass, but at least the prices were decent. There was no place to insert her credit card though.

When she walked into the small building, there was a man behind the counter, and the sheriff stood there talking to him. They both raised their eyebrows when she walked in.

"Um, hi!" She handed her card to the man behind the counter. "This is for gas for the little blue car out there. Where are your restrooms? It's been a long drive." Holly smiled at the two men.

The man behind the counter smiled shyly and pointed toward the back. "Right through that curtain, miss. And to your left."

"Thanks!" Above the dirty, yellowed curtain there was no sign that said "Restroom." She pulled the curtain back, stepped through, and opened the door to her left. There was no sign anywhere that marked this as a public restroom. Was that even legal? Flicking on the light, she locked the door, put the toilet seat down, and since there were no toilet seat covers, she laid rows of toilet paper onto the seat.

Holly was surprised at how clearly she could hear the conversation from the outer room. She thought it was because both men's voices were elevated.

"You wanted me to get married!" said the first man.

"Yes, but not to an Ungodly!" said the second with disgust.

"*She's* the one I want, and I'll turn her around. I promise, Joseph. I can do this!"

"What's so special about *her* anyway? Come on, Jared. There are plenty of women right here to choose from. Any of them would feel honored to be your bride."

"She *smiled* at me, Joseph. Not because I'm *your* brother, but just because I'm me. She smiled at *me!*"

"Meaningless, Jared. She smiled at me too."

"I want her, Joseph. I mean it."

"It's out of the question. She's one of the Ungodly."

"I'll give up First Rites," said Jared, the last words rising in pitch.

There was a short silence, and then Joseph said, "All right! I'll figure out something. Do you have one of those sticky notes? And a pen?"

Holly washed her hands, opened the bathroom door, pushed through the curtain, and walked to the counter. The sheriff had walked outside and was looking at her car. She smiled at the man behind the counter and said, "I'll be right back." He smiled but didn't say a word. His stare felt intense, and as she walked out the door, she shivered. The sheriff continued to walk around her car looking at it.

"Everything's up to date, Sheriff," Holly said.

He nodded solemnly and said, "I see that."

She opened the door of her car, reached in to release the gas cap cover, and closed the door. After unscrewing the gas cap, she pressed the unleaded button and slid the nozzle into her tank. Then she pulled the trigger back and set it so she could go back inside to get something to eat. As she walked into the building, she glanced back to see that the sheriff had stopped circling her car and was writing something down.

"Anything else?" asked the man behind the counter when she walked in.

"Yeah, some chips or something." Holly looked around the small room. There was a rack of chips and snacks, another rack of candy bars, and a cooler with soda, juice, and water in it. A mirror in the corner caught her eye. She noticed that the man was watching her every move. He probably wanted to make sure she wasn't shoplifting, although with such a small store, what were the chances of that, she wondered. Returning her gaze to the snack racks, she picked up a bag of tortilla chips and a Snickers bar, and walked to the counter.

The man behind the counter, tall and slim, with close cropped blond hair and gray-green eyes, was attractive, but the way he looked at her creeped her out. He added the snacks to her bill, handed back her credit card, and gave her the receipt. She signed it, said thanks, and pulled the handle of the door to open it.

"See ya later, beautiful," he said as she walked out the door.

"Fat chance of that," said Holly under her breath. The whole place creeped her out, and she wanted to get out of there as soon as possible.

The sheriff was standing by the door of her car when she returned to it. She replaced the nozzle into the pump and held up her receipt. "All paid for. I'm going to leave now."

"I'm sorry, miss." He stood with his hands crossed over his chest. "I need to see your driver's license and registration, please."

"What? Okay." Holly leaned into her car and pulled her wallet out of her purse. Then she opened the glove compartment and retrieved her registration, which she handed to him while she went through the cards in her wallet. She found the driver's license and held up her wallet for the sheriff to see.

"Please take it out of your wallet, miss." The sheriff held out his hand. He was a big man, resembling the man inside, but taller and bigger across the shoulders and chest. He had the build of a football player and the demeanor of someone who was overly enamored with his own self-importance. When she handed him her license, he nodded, walked to his car, and slipped inside.

Holly wondered what this was about. She hadn't done anything, and she needed to get back on the road if she was going to make it to Oklahoma before dark. And she really wanted to get out of this creepy place. Who knew what kind of wacky people they had in Texas? If she had only known then what awaited her there, she would have gotten into her car and taken her chances with a car chase. Instead, she waited for him to return.

"Everything seems in order with your license and registration—"

"Good, I—"

"*You interrupted me*," he said while gritting his teeth and speaking louder than he needed to.

Holly took an involuntary step back. "I—I'm sorry."

He shook his head and put her license and registration in his pocket. "Turn around and put your hands behind your back. I'm taking you in," he said sternly.

"For what?" said Holly, shocked.

The sheriff pointed to a small sticky note attached to the gasoline pump. In hand-written scrawl, it said, "*It is illegal under section 842 to leave the pump while refueling a car.*"

"That wasn't there before!"

He shrugged and moved his index finger in a circle. "It's there now. So turn around."

She didn't know what to do. She felt not only angry but scared too. The sheriff was scary, and the whole place felt sinister. But what could she do? While she was thinking, she hadn't moved.

The sheriff raised his voice again. "Miss, I'll give you thirty more seconds, and then I'll add resisting arrest."

"You'll what?" Holly said. The whole experience felt

more like a dream than a reality.

Grabbing her shoulder roughly, he turned her around, pushed her forcefully against the car, then pulled both arms behind her back and snapped the handcuffs on them.

"Ouch! You don't have to be so rough!" She shook her head. "I can't believe this is happening."

"Shut up and get in the car." He pushed her in front of him until they got to the car. Opening the door, he put his hand on top of her head while she got in, and then he slammed the door shut.

CHAPTER TWO

OLIVIA KEPT HER place in the book with a finger as she gazed out the window past the row of hedges to the house across the street. She took a deep breath and exhaled slowly, while her mind filled with pictures of the day she and Dean had driven over to Plenty, Texas, to scope it out before she started her novel.

Dean accompanied her to a camera store where they had bought two top-of-the-line GoPro video cameras. Although Dean had argued for buying a cheaper "consumer" version rather than the more expensive "professional" model, Olivia had insisted that she wanted the best. Honestly, with the family money that man came from, she didn't understand how he could sometimes be so cheap! Frugal, he called it.

When it came time to install the two cameras on the car, Dean insisted that if they drove through town in a red BMW, it would stand out. Better, he had said, to go in his truck. Olivia had thought about it and reluctantly agreed. She would have preferred the comfort of her BMW, but his truck wasn't *uncomfortable*—just not as comfortable as her car. So he installed one camera in each of the back windows behind the tinted glass. They were virtually invisible from outside the truck.

The drive over to Plenty was long but pleasant. Time was always pleasant passed with Dean. He made her laugh. He always made her laugh. No matter how bad everything might be, Dean always had a knack for making her feel better. That's the kind of man he was.

Olivia was eager to get the drive-through finished, but Dean insisted on seeing Carlos Vasquez—a friend of his in the Texas Rangers—beforehand. When they passed by the Plenty, Texas, exit sign on their way to Amarillo, Olivia gazed through the window longingly. But Dean wouldn't back down about talking to Carlos first. Carlos was forty, with jet black hair and kindly dark brown eyes. After they had a too long lunch with him, they were on their way.

Olivia couldn't wait to see Plenty after all she had heard about it. Suddenly, the exit was right in front of them, and Dean turned the truck onto it. It impressed her that the town even had an exit, but they had probably paid off someone in government to get it. Money talks—even for a cult with questionable values.

The outskirts of the town were a few miles from the interstate. As soon as she saw it, ideas flowed into her head—or maybe even before that. Yes, it was something that Carlos had told Dean while they were eating lunch. As they approached the city limits, Olivia, with a remote in each hand, started the cameras going. She didn't want to miss anything.

A gas station with a small convenience store on the right was the first building they saw. Carlos had told them that the whole town had been built only fifteen years ago, so the buildings all looked the same age. The sheriff's office—and she assumed the jail—wasn't far from the gas station. It looked small, maybe an office and two cells. The sheriff's car, parked out front, looked old with chipped paint, gray primer in spots, and a broken taillight.

As they drove down the street, five miles under the speed limit, Olivia noticed that the people they passed all glared at the truck—and none of them had a smile on their face. When they turned left to get to the main part of the town, there were women walking by with children in tow—each one with a man walking in front of her. Not one woman on the street was alone or alone with children.

They drove by the grocery store—larger than she expected, but not as big as a supermarket—and other shops lining both sides of the street. When they reached the end of town, Dean turned the truck around and drove slowly back.

He had been right about driving the truck instead of her car. She had seen at least eight other trucks that looked similar to Dean's, and yet their truck was still drawing everyone's attention. Imagine the spectacle they would have made in her red BMW! Dean had a good head on his shoulders. He was a good complement to her impetuousness. They made a good team.

On the way home, she couldn't stop talking about her story ideas to Dean. But he acted reserved and didn't seem receptive to any of her ideas. When she asked him why, he had said that maybe she should just leave the idea alone—write about something else.

Then the phone rang and brought her back from that day not so long ago when everything had started. "Hello?" Dean and the occasional telephone marketer were the only ones who used her landline, but she answered hello anyway. "Guess what, Dean? The book arrived! It looks beautiful! I've already gone over the formatting, and it's all fine. I've begun another read through, but now I'm thinking that I'll click the *Publish* button instead of waiting until I finish. . . . Yes, I'm absolutely certain that I want to do this. . . . Nothing's going to happen, Dean. You worry too much. . . . All right, I'll be careful. . . . See you later? . . . Good. Love you. Stay safe."

CHAPTER THREE

And They Threw Away the Key

THE SHERIFF LEFT her in the car and angrily jerked the building door open. It opened so far that it stayed open. Holly thought that after he threw her in the car he would climb in the front seat and drive her away. When he didn't, it gave her a chance to turn around and try to open the car door with her hands still bound behind her. But it must have locked automatically. She didn't know what she would do if she escaped, but she figured that she'd think of something. Scootching over to the other side of the car, she tried that door too, but it was also locked.

Sighing, she closed her eyes and bit her lip to keep from crying. She opened her eyes again and noticed that the car's front window on the side closest to the building—the side she was now on—was half open. Then she heard the voices from within.

"What do you mean you arrested her?" said a voice that

she now recognized as the man behind the counter, the one called Jared.

"You wanted her! How else did you expect me to keep her here for you?" asked the sheriff.

"Well, not like that! Now what do we do?"

"Jared, sometimes I think you have the brain power of a snail. The obvious, man! I throw her in jail, and you help her escape. Then she is indebted to you, and she'll do anything you want her to. Duh!"

Although the words might have made sense to her, she couldn't process them with the roaring in her head from the stress. Holly had never fainted before, but she thought this might be what it felt like. She forced herself to take long, deep breaths and barely noticed when the sheriff pulled the door of the building closed.

Inside the sheriff's car looked as dirty and dingy as the outside. The upholstery was split and worn in several places and the rug worn through all the way to the metal in spots. In the front of the car, the dashboard looked cracked and in need of a good cleaning. There was no sign of the modern technological devices that newer police cars had. Leaning forward, she was checking to see if there was even a radio, when the front door opened and the sheriff slid into the seat.

"What are you looking at?" He swung his hand around and backhanded her across the mouth.

Luckily for Holly, she had already started leaning back, or she would have felt the full brunt of the blow. As it was, she felt something dribbling down toward her chin. When she licked her lips, she tasted blood. Closing her eyes, she clenched her teeth, hardened her resolve, and forced herself to breathe.

It was a short drive to the sheriff's station. When they stopped, the sheriff opened the door, grabbed Holly's arm hard and pulled her out with one motion. Then he gave her a shove toward the door of the station.

"Walk, you!" he said.

She tripped, and without arms to balance herself, took a header onto the cement in front of the door. Again, without her arms to break her fall, her breasts hit the pavement hard, and her chin bumped and scraped the cement.

He pulled her up by her arm, which made it hurt even worse. "Next time I say walk, you *walk!*" Opening the door of the station, he pushed her inside, this time not so forcefully.

It was a two-room building, with one room as the office, and the second larger room with two small cells in it. The sheriff opened the door of the cell farther back, unlocked her cuffs, and then shoved her hard inside. She flew across the small room, tripping over the narrow cot and landing with her shoulder against the wall. Her arms, still stiff from being behind her, couldn't move quickly enough to stop her from hitting the wall. Sinking down onto the cot, she turned around to look at the sheriff who still stood by the door of the cell.

"Ohhhh," he said in a baby voice, "did the Ungodly one

hurt herself? Too bad. You'll have to be more careful next time, won't you?" Then he strode out, slamming the door behind him.

Holly's first impulse was to run to the front of the cell, bang on the bars and shout, "You can't do this to me!" But she had no energy for that. The only thing she had energy for was to curl up on the bed and sob so hard that she got hiccups. When she was all cried out, she pushed herself up with her good arm, sat on the cot, and looked around the cell.

It was six feet by ten feet with a cement floor, which looked clean, but nobody had swept it in a while. The cot, with a thin mattress stained and stinky, and a metal bucket in the corner were the only "furniture" in the cell. There was no pillow. Standing up, she tried flipping the mattress over, but the other side was worse. It was either sit on the cold cement floor or on the stinky cot. Reluctantly, she sank back onto the cot to assess her injuries. Her lip was swollen, her chin sore and sticky from blood, her shoulder hurt badly where she had whacked it against the wall, but her arms were beginning to lose their stiffness. Considering everything, she was alive, and pretty well.

Emotionally, though, she wasn't doing well at all. She had no idea why the sheriff had created that trumped-up charge to throw her in jail. What did he mean by Ungodly, and why did he treat her so mean? It's not like she had run over his dog or anything. Confused, and with her head still spinning with stress, she managed to fall asleep.

Several hours later, the door to the sheriff's office opened and awakened her. The sheriff stuck his head in. "I'm outa here now. Don't go anywhere. I'll see you in the morning."

Holly jumped up and ran to the front of the cell. "What about dinner? Don't I get something to eat?"

The sheriff laughed. "Girl, this is jail. You get nuthin'!"

Holly swallowed but forced herself not to break down and cry. "When do I get my phone call? I want a phone call! It's my right!" She regretted leaving her cell phone in the car, but he probably wouldn't have let her have it anyway.

"*Where* do you think you are? This is Plenty. Women have no rights here, and the Ungodly have even less." With that he turned out the light, slammed the door, and left her alone in the dark.

CHAPTER FOUR

Donuts and Coffee

IN THE MIDDLE of the night, Holly woke confused and reached for the lamp beside her bed. When the pain from her shoulder shot down her arm, she remembered where she was and why. No, wait. She still didn't understand why. Leaving the pump while refueling the car? Really? Was that the same as leaving the scene of a crime? The whole situation was laughable, and yet here she was, lying on a filthy, urine-soaked cot that stunk of stale beer in a jailhouse in the middle of nowhere. When she turned over, she realized that her whole body ached either from the fall on the cement or the meeting with the wall.

Moonlight filtered through the barred window outside her cell. Even if she could find some way to escape, where could she go? It was miles to the interstate and even farther to any other town. She knew the general direction, but nothing more. What if she got lost? She could die of exposure in this desolate place. And the worst part was that she wasn't due back at work for a week and a half, so no one would be missing her until then. Sighing, she wrapped herself into a fetal position again and tried to sleep.

A noise startled her awake, and the lights went on. Holly blinked her eyes and moaned from how sore she was.

"Rise and shine, pretty lady!" a bright voice said.

"What?" Holly moaned again and forced herself to sit up.

The man from the gas station stood outside her cell, holding a cup of coffee and a box of donuts. "I brought you breakfast. Here—" When she stood up and walked toward the door, he noticed her face. "What happened to you? Are you all right?"

She touched her hand to her lip and found that it was still swollen. Her chin hurt too. "Your friend the sheriff roughed me up. And he didn't give me anything to eat last night. I'm starved, but I need to use the bathroom first." She turned around and looked at the metal bucket. "Any chance I can use the restroom out there?"

He didn't answer right away because he was studying her injuries. Then he nodded and said, "Yeah, sure, let me go get the keys." When he returned and opened the cell, he said, "I'm sorry about all of that. I hope you're okay."

Holly stepped out of the cell and looked at him for direction. "No need for you to feel bad, *he's* the one who arrested me."

The man shrugged. "Yeah, well. It's out there to the

right. Come right back, though."

She had hoped there was a window in the bathroom, but there wasn't. It was surprisingly clean, and after she finished, she put the seat back up like it was and washed her hands. The man stood between the front door and the door to the cells to make sure she couldn't make a run for it, so she walked into her cell without trying anything. "Thank you. I appreciate that."

"You're welcome. Hey, my name is Jared, by the way." He handed her the coffee and donuts. "Better eat 'em quick, though, before Joseph comes in. He'll get mad that I gave them to you."

"Thanks so much." She carried them into the cell and sat down on the cot. After taking a careful sip of the hot coffee, she began opening the box of donuts. Then she looked up at him. "I'm Holly. Thanks so much for the food. I'm famished."

"Eat up. I'd like to stay and talk to you, but I better stand out front and watch for Joseph." Jared turned and walked out of the room.

Holly, afraid that the sheriff would come and she'd have to give up the food, stuffed down one donut after another. As she chewed, she looked around for someplace to hide one, but there was nowhere. She might be able to put one in her shirt, but if he caught her, then Jared probably couldn't bring her anything more. Better to eat as many as she could before he got there. She'd eaten half the box, when Jared called out from the other room.

"Here he comes! Hurry!" He rushed into the cell, took the box of donuts and the half-drunk coffee, locked the door, turned out the light, and closed the door behind him.

But it didn't close all the way. She could see some light leak in from the edges of the doorframe. And she could hear voices.

"What are you doing here, Jared? Didn't I tell you to leave the girl alone?" Then he must have noticed the food. "You didn't give her anything to eat, did you?"

"Of course not, Joseph. It's my coffee, and I brought these for you. I ate some of them," said Jared.

"You never bring me donuts. What are you doing here?"

"I just came to see her, all right? What'd you rough her up for? You didn't need to do that."

"Is that what she told you—that I roughed her up? I did nothing of the kind. I slapped her and accidentally hit her in the lip, and I gave her a couple shoves. It's not my fault that she fell on the cement and into the wall of the cell."

Holly could hear him laughing. She licked the sugar off her lips, rubbed her face to make sure no bits of donut remained, and secretly hoped that Jared didn't laugh too. He had at least been kind to her. She didn't hear him laugh, and she was grateful for that.

"It's not funny, Joseph. You didn't need to do that."

"I'm just giving her more reasons to want to get away. That will make it easier for you. That's all. I was doing you a favor." The sheriff—Joseph—laughed again.

"When can I do it?"

"Let's give her a few days to feel the pain."

"Just don't hurt her anymore, all right?"

"Come on, let's go outside."

Easier for Jared? What did that mean? And do what? She leaned back against the wall and started massaging her sore shoulder. Pain is right. Jared had left the lights off, but now sunlight was starting to stream through the window. So that was east. Now she had one more piece of information than she had before.

CHAPTER FIVE

A Wink and a Light

WHEN SHE HEARD the two men go outside, Holly took a moment to squat over the metal bucket. She didn't want the sheriff to find out that Jared had let her use the office bathroom, because then he would never allow her to again. There was no toilet paper by the bucket, but she didn't expect any either. When she stood up, pulled up her pants, and sat down again on the cot, she saw Jared's profile whisk past the window, and then she heard a vehicle start and drive away. One ray of light in this whole dark adventure. Holly didn't know what his motivation was, but he was being kind to her, and right now, that's all that mattered.

A few minutes later, the sheriff walked in and stood in front of her cell. "I'm not an idiot. I know Jared gave you coffee and donuts. So don't be expecting any other food or drink from me. You've already had more than you deserve."

He turned to walk away.

"Can I at least have some water, please? Please?" She had briefly considered pointing out that he hadn't given her any dinner, but decided not to mention it.

As he walked away from her cell and through the doorway, he said, "I'll think about it." The door slammed behind him.

Holly sat on the dirty cot with her back against the cell bars, and she wondered what she had done to deserve this. She had plenty of time to search her past for every inequity she might have ever committed, and several hours later, she decided that she was a pretty good person who had led a pretty good life, and there was no way on earth that she deserved this kind of treatment.

When the door opened, she turned her head to see the sheriff standing there grinning. "Here's your water! Catch!" Then he threw it on the floor and it landed outside her cell, just out of her reach. "Maybe if I have reason to walk down there later, I might kick it closer to you. Or—maybe not." Then he gave a quick laugh and slammed the door.

Although she felt thirsty, she decided not to even try to reach the water. Let him have his fun. She could always try to reach it later. When later came, she stuck her arm through the bars, but the bottle of water was too far out of her reach. She was about to try to stick her leg through, hoping its extra reach could snag the bottle, but then the door opened and the sheriff walked in.

"Can't reach it? Huh? Too bad. Well, maybe I can help."

He walked over and kicked the bottle toward the wall, as if he were trying to make a bank shot. It hit the wall and rolled in front of the other cell. The sheriff shrugged his shoulders and said, "Ah, well. Maybe I'll be a better shot tomorrow. Bye!" And he walked out the door.

It looked like it was farther away from her, but the way it hit the other cell actually made it closer. After moving the cot over, she angled her body on the cold cement, stuck her arm through and grabbed it. Holly moved the cot back into place and sat on it holding the bottle of water as if it were the most precious gem in the world. Two hours later, when no more light came through the window, she finally allowed herself to take a sip. It was the sweetest water she'd ever tasted. When you're not allowed to have something, it becomes a lot more valuable when you finally get it.

The donuts, even though she had gorged on them, didn't go very far, and her stomach complained about the lack of food. The water helped, but she still felt starved. If she only had the chips and Snickers bar that she bought before she was arrested.

Nothing else to do, she thought, so she lay back and tried to fall asleep. She was dozing off when the opening of the door startled her. Someone with a small flashlight walked toward her cell door.

"It's me. Jared. I brought you dinner. Sorry it's so late; I had to wait until I was sure Joseph wouldn't be going out again. Here. I brought you something to eat—a TV dinner —I'm not much of a cook. That's why I need a wife!"

As she took the Hungry Man dinner and a fork from him, she saw him grinning when he said that. But at the moment, her stomach was the only thing on her mind, so she thanked him, sat down on the cot, and started shoveling the food into her mouth. It was warm, not hot but still wonderful. "This is delicious! Thanks so much for bringing it to me."

The light from the flashlight shone on the TV dinner allowing her to see what she was eating, and she was grateful that Jared did that. But when a kernel of corn slipped behind the tray, and she had to tilt her head straight down, she realized that the light was really shining directly on her breasts, not on the dinner. She blinked her eyes, swallowed hard, and didn't say anything more.

Because she was so famished, the meal was gone in five minutes, and she stood up to hand him the empty tray and the fork. When he took the fork, he stuck it in his mouth, licked it clean, and winked at her. "See you tomorrow morning," he said as he walked out.

Holly couldn't help herself; she shivered all over with a mix of disgust and dread, and it was all she could do to keep her meal down. She had been feeling guilty and chiding herself for thinking that he was creepy when he was being so kind to her, but now she realized that her first impression was right on. Several deep breaths and hard swallows later, she forced herself to think about something different to get her mind off him licking her fork and winking at her.

CHAPTER SIX

DEAN FLIPPED HIS phone closed, exhaled hard, and tightened his lips. Then, unconsciously, he put his hand on his gun. Olivia was so nonchalant about the book, and he was so afraid for her. He already knew that she would not be cautious, and that scared him. She didn't understand what a volatile situation this was.

When they had stopped to see Carlos on the way to Plenty, Texas, and while Olivia was in the restroom, Carlos had told him about the woman who had escaped from the cult and managed to get to her sister's house in Houston. Less than a week later, she had mysteriously disappeared and had never been heard from again. The Rangers had marched into Plenty to investigate, but no one was cooperative, and when they left they didn't know any more than when they stepped into the place. They searched and found nothing. No one would answer any of their questions—the people were more hush-mouthed than a studious kid in study hall.

Then Carlos had told him about people passing through Plenty and never being seen again. Those were just anecdotal he said—no real evidence—but Carlos had still warned Dean to be careful. As they drove back west toward Plenty, Dean had told Olivia about the stories. She had laughed and said that it gave her the idea for the main plot of her novel. She was very nonchalant about the warnings and didn't take them seriously, remembered Dean. He hit the steering wheel with frustration and looked at his watch. He still had a few minutes before his break was over; and he was glad for the extra time which would give him a chance to calm down. But instead, his mind returned to that day.

When they approached town and saw the "Entering Plenty, Texas" sign, Olivia had touched the remotes to turn on both cameras, and Dean had immediately felt apprehensive. It may have looked like any other small town, but it didn't *feel* that way. Dean had been in the Texas Rangers long enough—and now in the Arizona Highway Patrol—to intuitively know when something *felt* wrong. And that town felt wrong. He had reached for the gun at his side and when it wasn't there, he had felt a small tremor of panic. Then he pushed the button to lock all the doors, while Olivia looked at him in surprise. As they pulled into town, her attention was filled with looking at everything and wondering what she could use in her book.

They drove by the gas station and the sheriff's office. Olivia didn't notice when the sheriff had slid into his car as they drove by and began following them—not even trying to hide it with a discrete distance. Dean had shuddered. As they drove by people on the main street, they all turned their heads with sullen faces to watch the truck pass. When Dean turned the truck around, he began running through scenarios in his head in case the sheriff pulled them over. Luckily, he didn't—but he did follow them all the way to the main interstate. And not until the sheriff was no longer in his rearview mirror, could Dean finally breathe freely again.

Olivia began chattering on and on about everything she had seen and how eager she was to view the videos for anything that she had missed that might be valuable setting information for her book. Dean had tried to talk her out of writing it, but to no avail. And he could hope that she wouldn't write it, but she was, after all, a writer, so he knew she would. When her publishing company declined to jump at her idea, he had tried to convince her that they were right, and it wasn't a good idea. But she still wouldn't listen. She said that after she wrote it, the publishing company would jump on the book. When they didn't, before he could even relax with relief, she had announced that she would self-publish the book. There was nothing he could do to convince her otherwise, and now she was about to release it to the world and ignore the possible consequences.

Of course she thought she was immune from any repercussions from the cult. The woman who had disappeared was just a woman of the cult—nobody knew her or knew of her. Who would notice? Olivia pointed out that she was a *New York Times* best-selling author and that she was too well-known for the cult to take a chance like that. Besides, she was two states away from the cult—too far from their area of comfort for them to come after her. And finally, she had argued, those people didn't read books anyway!

Dean had finally shrugged and sighed and given up. He resisted telling her that if they didn't read books, then they wouldn't know that she was a best-selling author. That woman—he loved her dearly and that's why he was afraid for her —could really be hardheaded and not listen to reason. It's something that he disliked and loved about her at the same time. She stuck by her convictions even though they were sometimes wrong. Who else had the strength to stand up for herself like that? Olivia was one of a kind. He had to find a way to keep her safe.

He radioed in that he was back on duty and drove off.

CHAPTER SEVEN

A Chance for Freedom

HOLLY HAD FALLEN back to sleep quickly after eating the TV dinner, and a few hours later the small flashlight awakened her again. Her stomach lurched when she realized who it was, but she didn't let on anything was wrong.

"It's Jared! I brought you breakfast again, but I didn't want Joseph to catch me here this time. Sorry it's so early."

"Do you mind if I use the restroom again, Jared?" Holly said as she approached the cell door.

"Oh, yeah, sure. Just a minute." He slid out the door and reappeared jingling the keys in his hand. "There ya go. Hol-ly."

The way he said her name—alone like that and accentuating both syllables—gave her the shivers again, and she had to keep swallowing when her stomach threatened to give up her dinner. She bit her lip and said, "Thank you" as she walked past.

"Don't turn on the light. Here, use this." He handed her the flashlight as he positioned himself between her and the front door.

Nodding her head, she stepped into the bathroom and locked it behind her. After lowering the seat, she sat on the toilet and tears sprang into her eyes, but she fought them off and wiped them away. There was no way she could let him see that she was upset. Everything had to look normal. Her first impulse was to stick the small flashlight in her mouth while she washed her hands, but then she realized that *he* had touched it, and the thought of it grossed her out. She laid it on the top of the sink trying to find a dry spot, and picked it up again after drying her hands. Then she unlocked the door and walked out.

He smiled when he saw her, and she averted her eyes and handed him the flashlight. "Thank you," she said and walked down the aisle toward her cell.

"Here's the coffee and donuts, Holly. I brought you some jelly-filled ones today. Hope you like them."

"Thank you very much, Jared. Jelly-filled are my favorites." It wasn't a lie. They were.

"I just want to make you happy, Holly. That's all."

The breath caught in her throat, and she hoped that it didn't make a sound. Holly took a sip of the hot coffee and a bite of the donut, and thought about Jared. He was creepy, but if she played along, maybe she could get him to do her bidding. "It would make me really happy if you could get me out of here." She smiled her sweetest smile at him, but it gave her a sour feeling in her stomach.

"Ha ha, that's a good one, Holly. But—you know—I'll see what I can do."

As she ate the donuts, she realized that the light was focused on her breasts again. If he got her out of here, he could shine the light anywhere he pleased. "That would be awesome, Jared. Really awesome. It would really make me happy to get out of here." She hoped she wasn't overdoing it.

"I better go now. Finish up. I need to leave."

She took a big swallow of coffee and took two chocolate sprinkled donuts out of the box. "I'll finish these in a second —if that's okay." If she acted submissive to him, maybe he would help her get out of here.

"Sure, Holly. Thanks for asking. I brought them for you. Just don't leave any crumbs on the bed for Joseph to see."

"No, I won't do that. No worries."

"Bye now. I'll try to stop by later if I can."

"Thanks so much for everything, Jared."

When he closed the door behind him, again it didn't close all the way because she could see his flashlight through the side of the doorframe. She heard the front door close and the car engine start, and then she heard the car drive away into the darkness. Slowly, she finished eating the donuts, and afterward, since it still wasn't light yet, she ran her hand along the top of the cot to make sure that no sprinkles had fallen there. Then she remembered—she hadn't lifted the seat back up in the bathroom. Maybe the sheriff wouldn't notice.

But he did notice. When he opened the bathroom door, she heard him say, "What the—" and then he immediately stomped back out again. Then she heard him on the phone. "Jared? Were you here? What I really want to know is if you used the toilet in my office or if you let that Ungodly girl use it. . . . Tell me the truth. . . . You're lying and I know it! . . . Jared, I'm warning you. If I catch you here again, I'm going to start locking the front door. I'm serious. . . . You promise? . . . All right then. Good-bye." Then she heard him walk back into the bathroom and close the door behind him.

The rest of the morning throbbed by with Holly wondering what indecency would happen to her next. The sheriff didn't even come to see her until mid-afternoon. She had been nursing the bottle of water he had "given" her, but it was finally empty, and she was thirsty.

"Looky what I've got! Another bottle of water! I'm going to try to bank it right in there today. But if I don't"— he laughed—"you don't get any until tomorrow morning! So you better hope that I'm on my game today!"

"I'm hoping, I'm hoping," Holly said under her breath, without turning around.

"Here goes." He threw the bottle, banked it against the wall, and it rolled over and stopped in front of her cell.

Holly looked at the bottle but didn't move toward it until she heard his footsteps rushing down the corridor toward her. She jumped off the cot and kneeled down to grab the bottle, but he had already kicked it away. When she looked up at him, he shrugged.

"Sorry. I fouled myself."

Then he turned around and walked out of the room, leaving the bottle so far out of her reach that she didn't even try to get it. She sank back onto the cot, grabbed the empty bottle of water, and tried to squeeze another drop out of it, but she had already gotten the last drop an hour before.

Lying in bed, trying to sleep, all she could think about was getting out of there. She finally fell asleep and woke hours later, hungry and thirsty. It was late. Later than Jared usually came for dinner, so she guessed that he had finally listened to the sheriff and not returned. Tossing and turning didn't help quiet her stomach and her dry mouth. The stench of the bed wasn't conducive to sleeping anyway.

An hour later, she heard a car's engine outside. Then the door opened, the flashlight appeared, and she rubbed her stomach, grateful for the food he would give her. But when she went to the cell door, he had one hand behind his back, but no food.

"You're looking for dinner, right? No dinner. But I have something better for you!" He brought his hand out from behind him and jangled the keys. "I'm breaking you out of here. Come on! Let's go!"

CHAPTER EIGHT

Change of Scene

JARED UNLOCKED THE cell door and held out his hand for Holly. She took it without thinking, although she did think that he held on a little too tightly.

Pulling at her, he said, "Come on. Hurry before Joseph comes in. I'll take you to your car."

She glanced at her watch and didn't think that the sheriff would be coming in the middle of the night. But she figured that anything was better than being in that stinking cell. It was a thought that she would later come to regret.

Jared led her around the building to his vehicle. It was a big, white truck with 4 x 4 written on the side of it in red letters. It had a backseat and oversize tires. "Come on! Get in!" He opened the door for her, and she had to climb into it to reach the seat. "I'll take you to your car. Let's get out of here!"

Before he even put his seatbelt on, he pressed the button

on his door handle that locked all the doors. Holly didn't think much of it, because it was something that she always did whenever she got into her car. Then they drove down the street until she noticed the gas station and mini-convenience store on the left. Jared pulled into the driveway of a house directly across the street from it. There was her car parked at the far end of the sloped driveway, right in front of a shed.

She grabbed the door handle, but the door was still locked. Looking at her with an odd expression on his face, Jared shut off the engine and hopped out of the truck. As her door unlocked, Holly jumped out, ran to her car, and pulled the handle to open the door. It was locked.

"Where are my keys?" Concerned about this turn of events, she turned to face him.

"Inside. Come on. I want to show you my house."

"I'd really like to get going. I don't want to get caught by the sheriff again."

He put his arm around her in a tight grasp pulling her toward him. "It's the middle of the night, Holly. He won't even be up for hours. Come on, I want you to see my house. It's the least you can do after I broke you out of there."

This was a contradiction that she couldn't ignore. When they were leaving the jail, he had told her to hurry before the sheriff came back. Now, suddenly, the sheriff was no longer a threat. Using only her peripheral vision so he wouldn't see that she was looking for an escape route, she tried to find a way out. She shifted her shoulders to get out of his grasp, but he held onto her too tightly.

"*I said*, come in and see my house."

His voice had suddenly come to mirror Joseph's. Holly knew she was in trouble, but he grasped her so tightly, there was no way to get away and nothing to hit him with. He pushed her in front of him toward the side door, and she had no reason to resist. It would do her no good. She was at his mercy.

Pushing her into the house, he gave her a shove and bolted the door behind him without turning around. "Don't try to run, Holly. I'm fast. I don't want to hurt you."

Holly took a deep breath, blinked her eyes, and looked around. They were in his kitchen, which was decorated in pink and yellow. It was cleaner than she would have expected. No dishes in the sink or on the counter, and everything arranged neatly. There was a bright yellow clock on the wall in the shape of a hen. It's eyes moved back and forth as it ticked the time away. The appliances looked modern and brand new. The one thing missing, she noticed, was there was no dishwasher.

"This is my kitchen."

"I can see that," she said with disgust.

"Walk in there." When she hesitated, he grabbed her wrist. "Look, Holly. We can do this the easy way or the hard way. But I *will* get what I want. Now walk in there." He pointed past the square, wooden table and into the formal dining room.

When he released her wrist, she walked in front of him

and saw his living room. Again, everything was in perfect order. It had two couches, two plump easy chairs, a rocking chair, and a coffee table. The couches and easy chairs, upholstered in a neutral beige plaid, all matched the big, dark beige pillows on them. Holly saw several doors in the room, which made her think that it was an awfully big house for one person. Maybe his family was away, and he brought her home for some kicks while they were gone. Focusing back on the living room, she swept her arm around the room. "No television?"

"We don't listen to that garbage in Plenty. No one here has TV."

"Hmmm. No TV and no dishwasher. How provocative."

Jared stayed silent, so Holly shook her head and looked around. With no way to escape, she thought the best way to get out of her dilemma was to get through it. "All right. Let's get this over with. Where's the bedroom?"

He looked at her with disbelief in his eyes. "The *bedroom?* No, go through that door there, turn on the light, and walk downstairs."

She walked through the formal dining room with the large, rectangular table. Feeling confused, Holly opened the door and looked downstairs at a finished basement. She stepped down carefully and found herself in a bright room with a red and white tile floor, a small kitchen table with a red and white checked tablecloth, and four wire chairs with red cushions. To her right was a couch and easy chair at the end of the large room. Both of them were white with red trimming. On the near wall were sliding doors, and behind one of the doors that was slightly ajar, she could see a washing machine. The room was wallpapered with brightly colored dancing fairies that you might find in a child's room. On the wall at the far end of the big room was a sliding door with vents on the bottom that probably housed the furnace and water heater. On the walls to the right and left of the heater compartment was a door on each side of the room.

Pointing to the door to her left, Jared said, "Through that door is the bathroom. You need to use it? There's no window."

"Duh! This is a basement." She thought about locking herself in, but to what avail? It would only make him angry, and she didn't need that. Her fear had given way to resignation, so she shook her head.

"Then go through that door," and he pointed to the one across from the bathroom.

Holly stepped through the door and felt for the light switch. When she switched on the light, she found a room painted pale blue and a double bed with a brass headboard and footboard. The bedspread was dark blue with cartoon characters on it. There was a small nightstand with one drawer next to the bed with a clock and a dark blue lamp matching the bedspread. On the wall above the bed was a picture of a sailboat tossed about on stormy seas.

"Get on the bed, on your back." When she got on the bed, he said, "Raise your arm up here." She raised her arm, and he attached a pair of handcuffs from the headboard to her wrist.

"You can't get out of here except through the door at the top of the stairs. And I can lock it, but I think we'll leave it this way for today. You can call me if you need me."

"If you can lock me in, then why do you have to do this?" She nodded to the handcuffs.

He straightened up and glared at her. "To show you that I'm your Lord and master."

She closed her eyes and exhaled in a huff. "So I suppose you're going to rape me now."

Jared looked at her, horrified. Then he took her hand that was in handcuffs and held it in both of his. A slight smile appeared on his lips. He shook his head and said, "*Rape* you? *No*, I'm not going to *rape* you. I'm going to *marry* you."

CHAPTER NINE

OLIVIA LOVED THAT part about Jared wanting to marry Holly. She remembered when Dean read it for the first time, and how he had looked up with this shocked expression on his face. "I bet I know exactly what part you are reading now," she had said.

Dean had put the book in his lap and looked up at her. "I can't believe you did that! Although you foreshadowed it earlier, it was totally unexpected." Then without another word, he picked up the book and continued reading.

A little while later, Dean looked up again, his face stern. He shook the book at her. "I don't like this. I'm not even sure that it sounds realistic."

She smiled at him. "Wait until you read further, and then you will understand everything."

Abruptly, he looked at his watch and stood up with his finger holding his place in the book. "I have to leave for work. But I don't like where it's going." He opened the book, grabbed the corner of the page, and was about to fold it over until Olivia gasped. Looking up sheepishly, he shrugged his shoulders and reached for the bookmark on the table. Dean was a page-bender, and no matter how many times she had reminded him, in a moment of excitement he still resorted to bending the page rather than reaching for the bookmark. Olivia was absolutely obsessive about not bending book pages—not to mention on her own book! There were two kinds of readers in the world: page-benders and bookmark-placers. Dean was the former, and Olivia was firmly the latter.

When Dean put the book on the table, Olivia stood up. "Don't you want to take it with you? I know you don't like to read when you're on break, but when you get home tonight?"

Dean shook his head. "No, you know me. I'd be up all night reading it, and you wanted to go to the museum early tomorrow." He smiled at her. "I can wait to see if it all works out to my satisfaction when we get home tomorrow." Giving her a quick peck on the lips, he turned and walked toward the door.

"Stay safe, Dean. I love you."

"Love you, too, sweetie." And he disappeared out the door.

Olivia smiled at the memory of not so long ago and went back to her reading. A few pages further into the chapter, she frowned and set the book in her lap. No, this isn't right, she thought. She'd already read it—over and over again. The only item that needed changing since the last proof copy was a small tweak in the formatting, which she had already checked when the book first arrived. After checking it again carefully to make sure she hadn't overlooked something in her haste and excitement, she nodded her head and made up her mind.

She put the bookmark in the book, stood up, and walked into the bathroom to check her makeup. Olivia powdered her face, put a dash of rouge on both cheeks, touched up her lipstick, smiled at her reflection, and returned to the living room to retrieve the book. She didn't need it for what she was about to do, but she liked having it beside her.

Sitting at her desk in the office, she began clearing off the papers that Dean had left there. He could be a little messy at times—a sweetheart, but a messy sweetheart. Olivia sighed. But he was her sweetheart, and she didn't mind cleaning up after him. At least he didn't leave his socks and underwear on the floor when he stayed over!

When she had cleared the desk to her satisfaction, she placed the book next to her and smiled at it. *There's a Darkness in the Light* by Olivia Vandermeer. It was silly that she felt this way. She already had many books published traditionally—by a big publisher. But this was her first book that she published herself—Indie publishing, they called it. So it was a completely different process than having a publisher do it.

Initially, when her publisher had declined interest in the book because of its subject matter, it had disturbed her. But after deciding to publish it herself and going through the whole process, she found that she liked the freedom it gave her. She could add or subtract material anytime she wanted —she sometimes had to pay for the changes, but she still had the freedom to do so. And she could make sure and double sure there were no mistakes or typos. The book was hers, completely. That gave her a better sense of belonging to the book than when she handed it over to the publisher to do the work for her.

Involuntarily, she picked the book up and hugged it to her. It was all hers, and except for the small amount of royalties that Amazon and the other online retailers charged, all the profits would be hers. Nodding her head, she put the book back on the desk and turned on her computer.

A minute later, Olivia signed into the self-publishing website and looked at what they called the dashboard. It had one item on it. Her as of yet unpublished novel was the only one listed there. If everything went the way she planned, she might decline to use the services of the big publishers any more and do everything herself. That is, unless they offered her a big contract—maybe one where she could keep the eBook rights. Otherwise, she might just continue like this. It wasn't that difficult.

She clicked the *Publish* button, signed off the site, put the computer to sleep, and walked back to the living room to continue reading her book. Life was good.

CHAPTER TEN

That's What Wives Are For

IT WAS STILL the middle of the night, and when the roaring in her head finally subsided, Holly managed to fall asleep. Hours later, she awoke and looked at her watch. It was morning. Her arm ached from being stretched over her head. Trying to get in a position to lessen the pain didn't work and ended up making the pain worse. And then she realized that she had to use the bathroom, and she had to use it bad.

"Jared! Jared!" she called. Five minutes later when she had not received a response, she called out again, "Jared! Come downstairs! I need you!" But he still didn't show, and she couldn't hear any movement upstairs.

Fifteen minutes later, after calling out to him every five minutes, her bathroom problem had gotten worse. She had her legs crossed in a tight knot, and she wasn't sure she could hold it much longer. There wasn't even a bucket in the room that she could use, if she could even reach it.

Her cries to Jared took on a more desperate tone. "Jared! Please! You said you'd come down if I called you! Please! Jared!"

She had to go so bad that she was beginning to feel sick to her stomach. Thoughts of what he had said about marrying her brought bile into the back of her throat. Then she heard the upstairs door open and close. "Jared! Please! Don't do this to me!"

He must have heard the pleading tone in her voice because he ran down the stairs and into her room. "What's wrong, Holly? What is it?"

"Please unlock me. I have to go so bad!"

Without another word, he pulled his keys from his pocket, unlocked the handcuffs, and released her. She ran out of the room and into the bathroom. The seat of the toilet was up, so she kneeled down, put her head over the bowl, and vomited, but it was mostly dry heaves because she hadn't eaten anything since the donuts more than twenty-four hours before. Her stomach hurt when she finished, and after flushing the toilet, she sat on the seat and relieved herself.

When she stepped out of the bathroom, Jared was nowhere to be seen. The door at the top of the stairs was open, but she didn't have the energy to even walk up there. She sat back down in the bedroom, noticing that the handcuffs were gone. It would be a blessing if he didn't use them on her again. Sighing, she leaned back on the bed, willing the pounding in her head to go away.

Holly heard Jared coming down the stairs, but she didn't sit up. She lay there in a daze until she heard his voice.

"Come on, Holly, breakfast. That's where I was. I'm so sorry."

She heard a kitchen chair scraping on the tiles, but she still didn't move. Although she was starved, with everything that had happened in the last few hours, she had no energy to stand up and walk in there.

"Holly?" The chair scraped again and footsteps came toward her. Then Jared appeared in the doorway. "Are you all right?" He stood above her looking down.

"If you can call everything that's happened to me in the last few days *all right*, then I guess I am. I'm too weak to sit up."

Jared walked over, took her hand gently, and pulled her to a sitting position and then to a standing position. "Okay now?"

When she nodded, he put an arm around her and led her out of the room and over to the kitchen table. On top of it sat a box of donuts, two tall cups of coffee, one small bottle of orange juice, and some paper napkins.

"I appreciate the food, Jared, but is this all you eat? This junk?"

He shrugged and smiled. "It's why I need a wife."

Holly refused to let the roaring come into her head again, and despite herself, she said, "Bring me some eggs and bacon and some oatmeal and I'll cook for you. And if you're planning to serve TV dinners again tonight, bring some chicken and a vegetable instead, and I'll cook dinner too."

He beamed at her. "I knew you'd make a good wife. The minute I saw you, I just knew."

She had to swallow hard to keep the bile from coming back into her throat, and she drank a sip of coffee. Opening the box of donuts, she pulled out a jelly-filled one and took a bite. Without looking at him, she reached for the orange juice and asked, "Is this yours or mine?"

"Yours! It's too healthy for me, but I thought you might want it!"

He laughed, but she didn't respond. After pulling the top off the orange juice, she took two or three swallows and put it back on the table. Holly tried focusing all of her concentration on eating the donut, savoring the sweet taste in her mouth and not thinking about what horrors the future with this man might bring.

"Listen, I need to leave this morning for a short while, but after that, company is coming over. They'll bring you some new clothes, and we'll talk about our plans for the future."

She didn't want to answer, but she said, "Ours?" in a disdainful voice.

"Yes, ours! You'll cook and clean for me, and I'll treat you very well. You'll have children, and we'll be a family."

"And all this without my consent?"

"Oh, I think I'll bring you around to my way of thinking pretty quick. I'm pretty persuasive, you know."

"And then we'll live happily ever after?" she asked.

He looked at her with a serious expression on his face and said, "Yes, we will. I really think we will." And then he turned and as he walked up the steps, he said, "See ya later, alligator!"

CHAPTER ELEVEN

BY THE TIME Dean had parked the patrol car, filled out his paperwork, and said his good-byes, his mind was made up. He knew what he had to do.

After turning the key and starting the truck, he opened his flip phone and called Olivia. "Hi, Sweetie. . . . I was wondering if you've begun dinner or not. . . . Great! I'd like to take you out to celebrate your book! . . . You what? I thought you were going to wait until you had finished reading it. . . . All right. . . . I'm going home to shower, and I'll be there soon. . . . Love you, too. Bye."

Dean put both hands on the steering wheel, let his head sink to his chest, and sighed. She had already clicked *Publish*. He was hoping that during their celebration dinner he could talk her out of it. Now it was too late. She'd never unpublish after seeing those sales rolling in. He shook his head, put the truck in drive, and headed home to shower and get ready.

Later, as he drove toward Olivia's house, he thought about the night she had decided to write the book. Even after all this time, he still blamed himself. He had worked swing shift for a friend that night, but Olivia still wanted him to come over afterward. It had been a rough shift with some minor trouble. Nothing really dangerous, but enough to get his adrenalin working overtime. They sat on the couch watching television, and Olivia wanted to go to sleep. But he felt too revved up, so he continued flicking through the channels with the remote—Olivia's head resting on his shoulder.

He had thought that she had closed her eyes and was almost asleep. But as he hesitated on one channel before clicking to the next, she had suddenly sat straight up and asked him to go back. "Turn it up! Turn it up!" She pointed to the set.

It was a documentary on the cult that lived in Plenty, Texas. They had built the whole town from the ground up fifteen years ago. Now two thousand people lived there— every single one of them believing the same crazy ideas. After five minutes watching the show, Dean was ready to turn the television off, but by then Olivia was fascinated. She motioned him to go to bed without her and moved closer to the set. He had stood up to go, but felt something unusual in the air and decided that he should stay. It had been a funny feeling, similar to the feeling he got when there was an unknown danger around.

The show lasted two hours, and although Dean had to work the morning shift, he had sat there with her the entire time. Olivia was transfixed and didn't say one word while she listened to the narrator and watched the minimal footage that they showed. When it was over, she flicked off the set and turned to him.

"That's just crazy. I'm going to write a book about it."

"Olivia, you saw the credits. Someone has already written the book. That's what they based the documentary on."

She shook her head. "Not nonfiction, Dean. Fiction! More people pay attention to fiction. With nonfiction—even a visual medium like film—they're somehow separated from it. When they read a novel, it's like they know the characters—which instantly makes them invested."

He had felt his skin crawl with trepidation then, and he felt it again now as he drove to her house. No matter what he had said, he could not change her mind about writing the book. Even when the publisher refused the idea, she wouldn't let it go. And from that moment when she had asked him to turn up the sound until the present moment, Dean had blamed himself for not going to sleep when she had first asked. Any repercussions from her writing the book would be on him. So he had to keep her safe.

Pulling into the driveway behind Olivia's red BMW, he turned off the engine, crossed over the grass, and walked in the front door. "Hey, Sweetie, you ready?"

"I'm touching up my makeup," Olivia called down.

"Honey, your makeup is always perfect!"

Then she appeared at the top of the stairs smiling down at him. She had on a gossamer pink blouse with a plaid skirt that came to her knees, so as not to hide her beautiful long legs. Her long, blonde hair, that she normally kept tied back, was loose and sweeping over her shoulders just as he liked it. Olivia still took his breath away.

She walked slowly down the stairs and when she got to two stairs above him, he grabbed her and swung her around. "Hi, handsome," she said. Her arms were around him, and her eyes sparkled into his.

"Hello, beautiful." Dean put her on the floor where her eyes were almost even with his. "Have I told you lately how much I love you?"

"Yes, but you can tell me again anyway."

Dean laughed. "How about if I tell you in the car? I'm hungry."

He watched as Olivia glanced in the mirror and unconsciously touched her hair as she walked by. Then he opened the door for her, and they walked out toward his truck.

Dean drove them to their favorite seafood restaurant, The Wharf. It was a little dive on the other side of town that had the best steak and lobster that he'd ever had. It was their special place. During dinner, Olivia went on and on about how excited she was that she had released her book, so Dean didn't have the heart to say anything to her about changing her mind.

When they were sharing the key lime pie that they always had for dessert, he finally had to bring it up. He shrugged and said, "You know, Olivia, I was going to try to talk you into changing your mind about the book"—he shrugged again —"but after seeing how excited you are about it, I know that I can't." Dean took her hand. "But please be careful and don't do anything reckless."

Olivia put a spoonful of the delectable pie into her mouth, closed her eyes, and nodded. "Dean, I wouldn't do anything reckless. But after watching how meager my sales were today, I realized that I have to do something more."

"It's only the first day, Olivia. Sales will pick up."

"I'm a best-selling author, Dean!" Olivia was always very

proud of that. "I've been thinking about it, and I know what I have to do." She put the spoon down and looked at him. "I'm doing some book signings!"

"I think that's a great idea." Dean took a spoonful of pie.

"In Texas."

Dean dropped the spoon and gasped.

CHAPTER TWELVE

Dress for Success

"Yeah, right. Happily ever after," Holly said aloud. She reached for another donut, since that was her only choice of food right now, and washed it down with another big gulp of juice. Jared had locked the door at the top with a deadbolt—she heard it slide into place. So there was no need for her to walk up there and try it.

After eating three more donuts and finishing both the coffee and the orange juice, she heard the door upstairs unlock. The footsteps coming down the stairs didn't sound like Jared's, so she turned her head to see who it was. Two women headed toward her. The one in front was in her mid-thirties and the one behind her was in her early teens. Both women wore their hair in a tight bun behind their heads.

Holly, even though she had been kidnapped and chained to a bed, was always the friendly sort, so she unconsciously offered them a smile. "Ah, you must be the company."

The girl in the back spoke first. "I'm Marina, and this is my sister, Susan. We came to dress you!"

"Marina, please, let me handle it," said the older woman, who had now reached the bottom of the staircase.

"I'm Holly. What do you mean dress me?" Then she noticed what they were wearing. Long skirts and simple blouses. The skirts were plaid, in pale shades of gray, brown, and beige, with solid color modest blouses. They looked like clothes you'd wear to parochial school. Glancing down at what she was wearing, Holly saw black skinny jeans and a bright blue sweatshirt with "You go, girl!" on the front. At least her white sneakers would pass muster.

"What size are you, Holly?"

"You didn't answer her question, Susan. We came to get you new clothes because what you're wearing isn't acceptable for living here."

"Marina, please, I said let me handle it," said Susan.

Holly shrugged. "Woman to woman?"—she looked straight at the older woman—"I don't want to live here. I want to go home. Any chance you could—"

"Whatever she says is lies, Susan. Don't listen to her." The voice from upstairs sounded oddly familiar, but wasn't Jared.

"I'm not listening, Joseph. I'm just trying to get her size."

The sheriff! What was he doing here, wondered Holly.

"That's Joseph," said Marina. "He's Susan's husband."

"Oh, Marina! You're impossible. All right, Holly, what

size are you? We're going to get you some clothes that are *appropriate*. And we'll have to do something about your hair as well."

"I'm size eight."

"Shoes?" asked Susan.

"Six."

"You done down there? Because if I'm taking you shopping, I want to get it over with," said Joseph from the top of the stairs.

Holly didn't look up, but she did notice that the girl was looking at her curiously. So she smiled warmly at her. She could use all the allies she could get, and one never knew in what form an ally would appear.

"Let's go, Marina. We're done here."

"I want to stay, Susan." The girl sat down in the seat across from Holly and took a donut out of the box.

"No, Marina. Come with me. Now." Susan was halfway up the stairs, but she turned around to look at Marina and motion her to follow.

"Let the girl stay," said Joseph from the top of the stairs.

"But, she—"

"I *said*, let her stay. And don't worry about the woman's Ungodliness rubbing off on Marina. The girl will never give her a chance to speak anyway."

Joseph and Susan disappeared, the door closed, and the bolt slid into place. Marina put her finger to her lips until she heard the outside door close. For more than an hour, Marina droned on about inconsequential topics of no interest to Holly. Then after a brief pause, Holly learned some valuable information.

"I thought Joseph would let me stay."

"Why would you think that?" asked Holly, curious.

"Because he doesn't like me. And I know that he doesn't like me because he tells me that all the time." Marina hunched her shoulders and shook her head. "He's mean. I don't like him either. He's probably going to hit Susan for talking back to him. He usually does."

"What's he doing here? What does he have to do with Jared?"

"Oh, you don't know? Jared and Joseph are brothers. Jared's the nice one though. I was hoping that he'd want to marry me, but even if he did, Joseph wouldn't let him because he doesn't like me."

"Married? How old are you?"

"Fourteen. But as soon as I get my period—which means I'm a woman—I'm eligible to get married."

"That's crazy. You know that Jared wants to marry me, right?"

"Yeah, I heard. Joseph hasn't stopped talking about how stupid Jared is for wanting to marry you."

"And you know that I don't want to marry him?"

Marina shrugged. "Yeah, so what?"

"What do you mean, so what? Don't women have a choice here?"

"No, silly, of course not. Women are chattel. We don't get to choose anything! Where did you come from, anyway, that you don't know *that*? *Everybody* knows that!"

"I came from Arizona. We don't live that way out there or almost anywhere else—at least in the United States."

"How'd you get here, anyway? I was wondering how Jared found you."

"I drove here in my car."

"You drove? You have your own car? Oh! Women aren't allowed to drive here. They're completely dependent on the men."

"And you *like* that?" Holly asked incredulously.

"Liking has nothing to do with it. It's the only way for women to get to the Promised Land. We have to obey the men, do *everything* they say, have babies, and submit to the procreating."

"The procreating?"

Marina slapped her hand on the table and smiled a big grin at Holly. "Surely they have procreating where you come from! It's the way a man impregnates a woman."

"Something tells me that's not all there is to it here," said Holly slowly, narrowing her eyes.

"When a man gets married, he has First Rites—that means that he has sex with his wife first. If she gets pregnant right away, then as long as she continues to get pregnant after having each baby, then the man gets to keep her all to himself. But, if a woman doesn't get pregnant that first time—because the more babies a woman has the more she is honored when she gets to the Promised Land—then the other men procreate with her. Ten a day for as long as she's ovulating—we call it ovo."

"Ten men a day?" Holly caught her breath.

"Yes, ten."

"But, why?"

"Simon Banks, who started Children of the Light—"

That got Holly's attention. "Wait. I thought Children of the Light were the Quakers."

"Oh, sorry. Simon always explains that to people who don't know. I should have mentioned that before. Simon felt that since it describes our people so well, that the Quakers wouldn't mind sharing it. But we're not like the Quakers at all.

"Anyway, Simon says that expanding our population is the most important thing, because the more people we have, the more power we'll have. And the more power we have, the more people we can convert. So it's extremely important for all women to keep having babies—as many as they can. Besides, having babies is the only way for women to get to the Promised Land—well, that and being obedient."

Holly shook her head, unbelieving. But before she could even start to process this information, Marina continued.

"Back to the ten. The first is always Joseph because he's the Town Chieftain, and next is Jared, because he's Joseph's brother—that's where Jared is now, procreating—and then other men sign up. If eight other men don't sign up, then Joseph assigns them. And if they don't do what he says, then there's punishment."

"Am I hearing right? Ten men every time a woman

ovulates?" She leaned forward, shaking her head.

"Yes, every time and every day. Oh! Are you thinking of me? It won't be ten men for me. For the first year after a girl becomes a woman, it's only five men a day."

"You mean after you have your first period and you're ovulating, five men will have sex with you that first time? Ouch."

"Yes. What do you mean ouch?"

"The first time hurts and with five men on the same day, that's going to hurt a lot."

"Oh, it's just part of being chattel. I won't mind, really. It's how I'll get to the Promised Land. The part I won't like is that unless someone asks to marry me, *Joseph* will be my first."

Before Holly could answer, they heard the upstairs door close and voices upstairs. Marina jumped up and put her finger to her lips. "Shhh! Don't tell anyone that I told you about this!" She ran to the sliding door where the heater was and pulled a cord, then she motioned for Holly and whispered, "Shhh. We can hear every word from here."

CHAPTER THIRTEEN

THE NIGHT THAT Dean had taken Olivia out for dinner and she had sprung on him her plans to go to Texas for book signings, she knew he wasn't happy, but here they were. It was a medium-sized bookstore in Amarillo—the closest city to Plenty—because she thought that might generate enough publicity to get more people at the rest of her Texas stops. They were in the back of the store, surrounded by shelves, and a cluster of twenty-five seats in front of her, about half of them occupied. To her right and behind her was the fiction section T through Z, although none of her books were on the shelf. Stacks of them were piled in front and to the side of her, and more displayed prominently in the front window of the store.

The bookstore employees were running around getting ready for her presentation. Although Olivia had done hundreds of these book signings—okay, maybe it was just dozens—she always felt nervous until they began. Then she would launch right into her reading and the nervous jitters faded away as she immediately got her flow.

She had brought candy and cookies for the attendees

along with a bookmark that she put on every seat and some at the cash register. When she had asked Dean to help her set up, he just shook his head and continued walking around like a soldier at his post. Now he stood behind her, his eyes wary and watchful for any sign of trouble. The front side of the bookmark had the book's cover and its blurb, and on the back was a section entitled *If You're Interested in Joining This Cult*, and had several items listed, some funny, some horrifying, and every one of them inflammatory according to Dean. Olivia had insisted though.

When they were preparing for the trip and Olivia was picking out her clothes, Dean told her that for Texas, she would be fine in jeans and a western shirt. When he saw the dress she had picked out instead, he whistled and shook his head. "That's one of my favorites, Olivia, but your whole book is about the weird sexual proclivities of the cult. I don't think you want any sexuality to come across at all."

She had looked in the mirror, held the dress up to her and turned this way and that, but after he said that, she realized immediately that he was right, so she returned the dress to her closet. Now she wore one of the several pairs of conservative slacks that she had brought for the trip—all of them in pastel colors—and a demure blouse. Today's pants were lavender and her blouse was pale blue. Dean approved.

"Ladies and gentlemen!" The bookstore manager inter-rupted Olivia's thoughts. "Today we have with us Olivia Vandermeer, best-selling author, reading for us from her newest book, *There's a Darkness in the Light.* Welcome, Olivia!"

Dean gently squeezed her shoulder from his post behind her. He was the most supportive man that she had ever been with, and she appreciated him very much. Supportive but overly cautious. She could live with that.

Looking out at the audience, she saw that while she had been sitting there waiting, every seat had filled, and several people were standing at the back, all of them intent on hearing her every word. After much consideration, she had decided that the best part of the book to read would be the first chapter. She had wanted to distribute a handout that had another excerpt in it, but then she decided that it might divulge too much about the book, so she didn't.

Now she stood up briefly, greeted the audience, nodded her head and smiled, and sat down and began reading. There wasn't a sound in the whole place, and even people who stumbled noisily in from the street, quieted as soon as they heard her voice. Then they would silently wander to the back of the store and become enthralled with her words just like the rest of the people in attendance. Olivia had always felt that her words had power, almost a hypnotizing effect, and as she looked out at the audience, they confirmed her beliefs. When she finished the reading and said a few words in summary, she opened the floor to questions.

The first questioner was a young woman in the second row. "Was this a true story?"

Olivia shook her head. "No, it's just fiction. I made it all up."

"But it's based on that cult. Over there," said a man who motioned over his shoulder. "Right?"

"It's loosely based on that cult, yes. But the characters

are all from my very fertile imagination." She gave a brief laugh.

"I'd say you characterized those loonies pretty well." The man who spoke was an older cowboy-type standing at the edge of the crowd directly behind the last row of seats. "You're not from around here, are you?" Without waiting for a reply from Olivia, he pulled an unlit cigar from his western shirt pocket and pointed it at her. "You best be careful, missy. Those people are dangerous. My daughter, Mary, got herself involved with one of those men, and I haven't seen nor heard from her since. And I can't get past the town sign to go look for her." He cleared his throat and continued. "If they get you in their clutches, you'll *never* get out." He turned and walked away leaving murmurs behind him. Then he turned back and pointed the cigar at her again. "And don't think that because you're a best-selling author you're safe from their grasp. They're lunatics and willing to do whatever it takes to get whatever they want."

Olivia watched him walk away, noticing his expensive peacock cowboy boots. The murmuring continued and she had to clear her throat several times to get the crowd calmed down from the cowboy's frightening words. And yes, they were frightening. While this was going on, she didn't notice the two men doing a double take at the front window, entering the store, buying one of her books, and sticking one of the bookmarks inside it. But Dean did.

CHAPTER FOURTEEN

Revelation Dawns

"HURRY UP, SUSAN. I want to get out of here." It was Joseph's voice; then she heard footsteps approaching the basement door.

"Close it! Quick!" said Holly in a whisper, not wanting to get caught.

"No, wait," Marina whispered back. "I heard another car. It might be Jared."

They heard the outside door open, and a second later, Holly heard Jared say, "Hey, Joseph. Hey, Susan. Thanks for getting her clothes. I appreciate it." The lock turned on the basement door, but before Marina had a chance to pull the vent back in place, Holly heard Jared's voice again. "Wait, Susan. I have another favor to ask. Could you do some grocery shopping for me? Bacon, eggs, stuff like that?"

"I don't have time to cart her around all over town for

you, Jared. If you want her to do that, you can take her yourself." It was Joseph's voice followed by heavy footsteps, and the sound of the outside door opening.

"Fine, Joseph. I can do that," said Jared.

"And don't take too long about it. Who's going to man the gas station? It needs to be open," said Joseph.

"I'll hurry, Joseph. Don't worry about it."

"I *am* worried about it." Then he turned to Susan. "Susan, be sure to take loudmouth with you. She's been down there with the Ungodly long enough." Back to Jared, he asked, "Did you handcuff her to the bed like I told you?"

Marina looked at Holly with wide eyes, and Holly nodded. Then Marina looked at both of Holly's wrists to see if there were marks there.

"Yes, Joseph, I handcuffed her to the bed and told her that I was her Lord and master," said Jared.

"You idiot! You weren't supposed to *tell* her that you were her Lord and master, that's what she would have felt just by you doing it. This whole thing stinks, Jared. I'm sorry I ever went along with it."

"Joseph, you're so transparent. You went along with it because I said that I'd give up First Rites."

The front door slammed, Marina pulled the cord, and she and Holly returned to sit at the table as if they had never moved, just as Susan started down the stairs, her arms full of packages. "I need to leave again, so why don't you try them on while I'm gone to make sure they all fit," Susan said when she reached the bottom of the stairs. She handed the bundle of packages to Holly, who stood to receive them, and then Susan started back up the stairs. "Come on, Marina. We're leaving now."

"I want—"

"I don't care what you want. Joseph doesn't want you down here any longer. Besides, we're returning later to talk about the wedding. You can come back down here then. You don't need to be involved in that."

"Shouldn't *I* be involved in that?" asked Holly.

"Of course not," said Susan. "Come on, Marina."

Marina shrugged her shoulders and started up the stairs. Midway, she turned back around to Holly and held her finger to her lips. Holly nodded. A minute later, the door closed, and Holly heard the bolt sliding into place.

She carried the packages into the bedroom, placed them on the bed, and sat down beside them. Something that she had heard in the last few minutes bothered her, but she couldn't remember what it was. Going over the conversation in her head, it suddenly occurred to her. First Rites! It was something she had overheard at another time and another place.

When she was using that tiny, unmarked restroom in the gas station convenience store, she overheard Jared and Joseph having a conversation about *her*! And it was then that she had first heard the mention of First Rites. Jared had said that he would give them up if Joseph helped him get "her." And Holly knew now that they were referring to her. The roaring started in Holly's head again, but she forced herself to remember the second conversation that she had overheard—where Joseph explained to Jared that he would throw her in jail and then Jared would break her out, making her indebted to him.

The two men had planned the whole nightmare in advance! The roaring got louder, and Holly leaned back on the bed and tried to take deep breaths. She also tried not to think about it, because every time she did, the roaring started all over again. Finally, she got herself calmed down and sat up. Then the term "First Rites" came back to her—along with Marina's explanation—but instead of the roaring starting again, she burst into tears, accompanied by heavy sobs until she was gasping for breath. Calming herself down once again, she managed to stop the crying through more deep breathing.

Holly decided that she should try on the clothing to get her mind off the inevitable. There were four long skirts, six blouses, and one long, black dress. That was curious. What was that for? It was pretty, with some ruffles around the neck, but it was black! She liked to wear bright colors, but all of these skirts and blouses were in muted tones of earth colors, like the ones Susan and Marina had been wearing. What was up with that? Pawing around in the rest of the packages, she found two bras—too big, but workable—two packages of white cotton panties that were her exact size, two packages of white socks, one full slip, two half slips, and two white nightgowns with a soft ruffle around the neck and at the bottom of the long sleeves. A shoe box in one bag held a pair of black flats. She would have preferred low heels, but it wasn't like she had a choice here. Susan had done a good job. She'd have to thank her.

After holding everything up and seeing that it looked like it would fit, she decided that she should take a shower and get clean before trying everything on. When she was in the small bathroom earlier, she had seen the narrow shower stall and noticed the towels on the rack. Since no one was around, she undressed and walked into the bathroom.

Holly had always done her best thinking in the shower. As she scrubbed several days of grime off, being careful around her bruises, she allowed First Rites to come into her mind again. She hated Jared even more now that she realized what he had done to her by relinquishing First Rites. Marrying Jared was one thing. Consummating the marriage was another. It bothered her, but realistically, there had been a couple of times in college when she was drunk or stoned and had slept with guys that she really didn't want to sleep with. But ten men in one day while she was ovulating! No way! That was something that wasn't going to happen.

Her period had ended more than a week before her trip, so she expected that she might be ovulating any day now. She felt like a slight cramp was coming on even now. As long as the marriage wasn't today or tomorrow, then she should have a month to come up with a plan to get herself out of here before her next ovulation—or "ovo" as they put it. And as she turned the shower off, she made up her mind.

Ten men, including Joseph! There was no way she was *ever* going to allow that to happen. Her fists balled up unconsciously. She would do *whatever* it took to stop that from happening and to get away from this horrifying place. Then she wondered if there was a gun anywhere in the house.

CHAPTER FIFTEEN

DEAN HAD BEEN watching the crowd carefully when something at the front window attracted his attention. Two men were walking by, when one man hesitated and pulled the other man back to show him something in the front window. What was in the front window was a giant display of Olivia's books. They walked in just as the cowboy with the cigar was talking to Olivia. For Dean, it was like a premonition coming true right in front of his eyes. The two men bought the book, took a bookmark, and left before the cowboy turned around. Dean shivered, and he would have reached for his gun, but he already knew that he didn't have it with him. He patted the knife sheath by his side knowing he'd do anything to protect Olivia.

He set his jaw and put his hand on Olivia's shoulder. This was it. Now he knew for sure there would be trouble, but he didn't know how much or how soon. At least he was here to protect her, and he was grateful that he had gotten the time off. But Dean was always the one willing to fill in for someone else, so all he had to do was call in a few outstanding debts.

Olivia turned around when she felt his hand and smiled up at him. Then people crowded around her introducing themselves and asking her more questions. Dean sighed. He didn't have to watch the crowd anymore. What he had expected—the cult to find out about the book—had happened, and now Dean could relax, for today anyway. Plenty, Texas, wasn't far from Amarillo, but they still had to talk to the so-called Messiah about it, and by that time, he and Olivia would be safely down the road and in their hotel room.

He remembered back to the night they had seen the documentary. It had been followed by a frantic week with Olivia buying books and videos—anything she could find—on the cult and its leader, Carter Weeks aka Carter de la Luz, which in Spanish means of the Light. Carter of the Light was the monumental force behind the so-called Children of the Light church. Carter of the Light and Children of the Light —it had a nice ring to it—at least Carter thought so.

In a video they had watched on YouTube, Carter had given one of his precious few interviews right after he changed his name and started Children of the Light. He had a beatific expression on his face, with his eyes unfocused and his words little more than a murmur, as he explained how the light had come into him after an almost fatal bout of spinal meningitis. Carter described how he had woken up from a medically induced coma with an excruciatingly bright light coming into his eyes—the pain was so intense that he had cried out. And when the pain went away, he was completely healed, and he knew in his heart that he was the Messiah.

He said he didn't tell anyone at first, but he found that

when he finally did, they all nodded their heads and said, "Yes, you are the Messiah!" Those few people turned into dozens and the dozens into hundreds, and now not only Plenty, Texas, was under his control, but the new city that he was creating—that Olivia had alluded to in her book by having the leader of the cult out of town—supposedly called Plenty More in Oklahoma.

That video was in direct contrast to another they had seen on YouTube of two men who had run into him at a gas station and taunted him by bowing in front of him, laughing, and making rude comments. Instead of ignoring them, Carter had engaged the young men in a yelling match of obscenities—not very messianic. And that video had a note on the bottom of how Carter's followers kept managing to delete the video, but undaunted, the posters kept re-uploading it for everyone to see.

Basically, though, Dean thought, Carter was a lunatic with a lunatic fringe of followers. A bunch of losers banding together under the man's tyrannical dominance. And from what Olivia had read and shared with Dean, once he—or any guru-type individual—had the people's faith and allegiance, no matter how outlandish his demands, they would blindly obey, thinking that was their ticket to heaven.

Now that Olivia had come into their radar—and he was sure that she had—she and Dean had to be extremely cautious until they returned to Arizona, and even then, Olivia would not be safe. Although he knew that she would resist, he had to convince her to keep a gun. She already knew how to shoot—she and Dean had gone shooting before—but she had always resisted the idea of her own gun. On principle, she said. Principles weren't going to stop Dean from insisting that she have a gun now. It wasn't important before. Now it was urgent. Whether she liked it or not, he would get her a gun. The cult knew about her book, and it was only a matter of time before they would seek their revenge. And who knew what kind of revenge it would be? Dean shivered.

CHAPTER SIXTEEN

Cleanliness Is Next to Ungodliness

HOLLY WALKED OUT of the bathroom wrapped in one towel and drying her hair with the other. Susan and Marina were sitting at the kitchen table.

Without a word of greeting, Susan demanded, "Have you tried on the clothes yet?"

Holly walked over to the table while she rubbed her head and glanced up the stairs to see if they had closed the door. They had. "No, Susan, I haven't. I haven't taken a shower in several days because I was in jail for doing nothing"—she stopped rubbing long enough to lean down and put her face right in front of Susan's and look her in the eye —"and I felt gross. Now that I'm clean, I'll try them on. Is that all right with you?" She straightened up and walked into the bedroom without waiting for an answer.

"Yes. I'm glad to know even the *Ungodly* can be clean," said Susan.

Although Holly had already stepped inside the bedroom, she poked her head out. "Yeah, right! You *Godly* are the ones who kidnap an innocent woman off the street, throw her in jail for trumped-up charges, and toss in a little abuse on the side. If that's *Godly*, I don't want any part of it."

That seemed to soften Susan. Holly had her bra and panties on when Susan walked in and said, "Look. It wasn't my idea to kidnap you or to marry you off to Jared. I'm only doing as I'm told, which is exactly what you need to do if you know what's good for you. You're lucky that Jared isn't like Joseph. But he does listen to Joseph; so if Joseph tells him that you need a good beating, then you can bet you'll get one." She stopped and looked at Holly. "That bra is too big, isn't it? I can exchange it for you."

"No, I'm sure it will be fine. Thank you, though, for the offer."

"Anyway, do what Jared says, you won't get beat, and you'll end up in the Promised Land with the rest of us. It may be a man's world, but there are advantages for women here. No responsibility! All you have to do is cook and clean and have babies. Simple!"

Holly pulled the skirt up to her waist and shook her head. "That's not the kind of life I want, Susan." Looking down at the skirt, she added, "This fits perfect, thank you." She ran her hands along the sides of the skirt, found pockets, and stuck her hands in them. "Cool pockets too."

"Put the rest of them on to make sure they fit too. But do that later. I just need to see if the black dress fits." Susan leaned against the doorframe. "It may not be the kind of life you wanted, but it's the kind of life you've got. Believe me, Holly, there's no escaping this place, so don't even try."

It was the first time that Susan had used her name, and it touched Holly. Struggling to get the black dress on, she turned her back to Susan to let her zip it up for her. "What's the black dress for?"

"It's your wedding dress," said Susan.

Holly turned around quickly to look at her. "A *black* wedding dress?"

"Women wear black wedding dresses because we're all unclean."

"It has nothing to do with being a virgin then?" Holly wondered aloud.

Susan shook her head. "Nothing. But that's a moot point anyway, now that Simon had a new revelation that as soon as a girl gets her period, she immediately gets on the procreation list."

"So nobody around here gets married while still a virgin, huh?" Holly exhaled hard in disgust—not because of the virgin part, but because such young girls get on the "procreation list." The whole thing was sick. She had read about cults before, and having sex with young girls was a part of most of them.

Susan shook her head again. "Rarely. Only if they get married before their first period." She started walking out of the room. "Try the rest on and let me know if you need me to exchange any of them." As she walked past the table where Marina sat the whole time, uncharacteristically quiet, Susan said, "Marina, you stay down here with Holly."

Marina stood up. "I want to go up and help plan the wedding!"

"No, Marina, stay down here and keep Holly company." Susan started walking up the stairs.

Holly, still buttoning the blouse that she had just put on, walked to the bottom of the stairs and looked up. "Susan, shouldn't I be able to help plan my own wedding?"

Susan shrugged. "It's not allowed. Men plan the weddings, and women do what they say. If they say for you to crawl down the aisle on your hands and knees, then that's what you'll do." Then she walked through the upstairs door and closed it behind her.

Holly looked at Marina. "Crawl on hands and knees down the aisle? Really?"

"It's what Joseph made Susan do." Marina jumped up and ran to the sliding doors where the vent was. "I'll tell you why later. Come on! Let's listen. Oh! By the way, I only said that I wanted to help upstairs because if they think all I want to do is talk to you, they'll never let me. And since they usually don't let me do what I want, I've learned to often ask for something that I don't want to get something that I do!" She shrugged. "Although sometimes in my excitement, I forget!" She pulled the cord. "Shhh. Come here."

Holly smiled at the girl's resourcefulness and leaned in next to her. "Thank you, Marina. I appreciate you showing me this," she whispered.

"I like to listen, too!" Marina whispered back. "And our house is exactly like yours, so I'm sure that no one can tell from upstairs."

"The dress fits her perfectly," they heard Susan say. "I don't even have to hem it."

"Good. That's one less thing to worry about," said Joseph. "And I've spoken to Simon."

Marina leaned closer and whispered, "Simon Banks is the Messiah of the Children of the Light."

Holly stepped back involuntarily and looked at Marina. "What?" But before Marina could answer, she heard Jared's voice.

"How soon can he get here? I want to get married as soon as possible."

"There are things that have to be done, Jared," said Susan.

"He can come in two days or a month from now. He's going away and those are the only choices," said Joseph.

"Two days! Two days!" said Jared. Then they heard a sound like he was jumping up and down.

"Impossible," said Susan. "Too much needs to get done."

"Susan! If Jared wants his wedding in two days, *you* will help him with it! Do you understand?"

"Ouch!" said Susan. It sounded like she was knocked off balance. "Yes, I understand," in a voice so soft that Holly could barely hear her.

"I think you're an idiot for this, little brother, but if that's what you want, you'll have it. And Susan will arrange everything for you." And in a sterner voice, "Won't you, Susan?"

"Yes, Joseph," said Susan in a compliant voice.

"All right, it's settled then. I'll call Simon, and he'll be here in two days. In the meantime, Susan will take care of all the details for you, and oh, yeah, you wanted her to do some grocery shopping too, right?" Without waiting for an answer, Joseph continued. "This is time for a celebration, right?" Joseph sounded almost jovial, briefly. "Susan, go with Jared!" And then the front door slammed.

Marina closed the vent and the sliding doors, and she and Holly quickly sat down at the kitchen table as if they were there all along. They both glanced up at the basement door, but when it didn't open, Marina looked at Holly. "Two days." The girl raised her eyebrows. "I know you don't want to marry him. What are you going to do?"

"I don't have a choice, do I, locked down here? Unless you could help me—"

"I feel bad for you and all. We're all used to not getting what we want. But you're a stranger here, and although you're Ungodly, I feel bad, Holly, I really do. But if I helped you, Simon would excommunicate me, and then I couldn't go to the Promised Land."

Holly reached out and patted Marina's hand. "Listen, Marina. There are *thousands* of religions out there, and many of them—a lot of them—claim that the only way you can get to Heaven, or the Promised Land as you put it, is to follow *their* rules. But let's say there are only one thousand religions and that eight hundred of them say their way is the only way to get to Heaven. What are the chances that a benevolent God would only choose one *single* way to get into his Kingdom?"

"But God doesn't like women. That's why he makes it so hard for them to get to the Promised Land."

"God created man *and* woman. And he doesn't like one of his creations? I'm sorry. That doesn't make any sense to me."

Before Marina could respond, Holly continued. "And another thing—about the ten men a day. You know what they call that where I come from? It's called a gang bang. It's *gang rape*."

"But trying to procreate here isn't rape, because the women want to get pregnant any way that they can."

"But only because they think that's the only way to Heaven. Right?" When Marina looked down and didn't answer, Holly repeated, "Right? And what if *that's* not true?"

Then the door opened at the top of the stairs, and Susan called out without enthusiasm, "Marina, time to leave now. You're going home while I help Jared with the wedding plans."

With knitted brows and a serious expression on her face, Marina started up the stairs. When she got to the top, she turned around and nodded to Holly, but the serious expression was still there.

CHAPTER SEVENTEEN

In the Nick of Time

HOLLY SAT AT the table nodding her head and thinking. Susan had finally softened toward her, and the conversation with Marina had started the girl thinking. Right now, that's all she could hope for. Marina might not ever help her escape, but at least she had started the girl thinking for herself, and maybe someday, she'd find her own way to escape. Maybe that's why Holly was here now — to help the girl. Susan was probably too far gone, but Marina was still young enough that maybe Holly could make an impression.

Regardless of all that, thought Holly, what she needed to do now was try on the rest of those clothes that Susan had brought. Being locked in a basement wasn't very conducive to escaping, so the first thing Holly had to do was prove that she was ready to play the role of submissive female. That was probably her only way out of here. Anyway, it was the quickest. But she couldn't do it too quickly, or they might suspect something—a little at a time—but steadily submit more and more. In high school, she had taken drama and been in the school play, and she had been told she was pretty good. She could do this—she had to.

After trying on the remainder of the clothes and finding that they all fit her to perfection—except the bras—she tried on the black shoes. They were a little tight, but not bad, and she assumed that the only time she would be wearing them was for her wedding. Susan and Marina had both worn white sneakers every time she had seen them. Holly slipped on her own white sneakers and tied the laces. Then she walked to the other end of the big room and sank down on the couch.

Finally being able to relax after so many days filled with tension was just what she needed. She took a long, deep breath and closed her eyes. Relaxing felt good, but she'd like to have a book or magazine to read. And a radio would be good. She'd have to ask Jared to bring her a couple of magazines from the convenience store.

Some time later, Holly heard the basement door opening, and Susan called down to her. "Holly! Come up here." Holly climbed the stairs, but Susan stood at the top blocking her way. "Promise me that you won't try to run when you get up here. You couldn't get far anyway, with Jared right across the street. Not to mention that they've drained all the gas from your car. But I want you to give me your word."

Holly looked down, clenched her teeth, and held her

eyes tight shut, before she made up her mind and said, "Yes, I give you my word. I won't try to run when I get up there. Right now."

A slight smile flickered across Susan's face before she nodded and stepped aside to let Holly inside the main part of the house. "Jared took me to get groceries for you, and I wanted to show you where I put everything, so you wouldn't be lost in your own kitchen."

"It's not my kitchen, Susan."

"Maybe not, but didn't you tell Jared that you'd cook for him?"

"Yes, you're right. I did."

Before Susan could finish showing her where she had put all the groceries, and way before Holly could appreciate how huge it was of Susan to leave her free like that, Joseph burst through the door. He took one look at Holly leaning against the kitchen counter, and he grabbed Susan's wrist, spun her around, and slapped her hard across the face.

"How could you be so stupid to turn her loose up here? Get back to the station and help Jared finish making plans. You've done enough damage here!" He shoved her out the door, and Susan didn't say a word. "As for you, get your butt downstairs in the basement where you belong. I have to talk to you about something important."

Holly walked to the basement doorway and hurried down the stairs, holding an arm out in each direction for balance. She didn't know what Joseph planned to tell her or do to her down here, but she had a bad feeling about it.

And she wasn't going to give him the chance to push her down the stairs.

Joseph closed the door behind him and tromped after her. "Sit down at the table!"

When she did, instead of sitting across from her, he sat next to her. She held both hands in her lap and looked down at them. Maybe if she didn't make eye contact, he wouldn't want to hurt her.

"You're getting married in two days—on Monday." When he had paused and she didn't say anything, he said, "Aren't you going to give me any lip about that?" She shook her head. "Why not?"

Without looking up, Holly said, "I don't want you to hit me again."

Joseph smiled. "Good. I finally got some respect out of you. That's a good start." He leaned back in the chair. "So. You're getting married in two days, and you need to be on your best behavior. Can I count on you to do that?" Holly nodded her head. "No trying to escape, no telling everyone in the church that you don't want to be there. You need to act like a bride who's excited about getting married. Can you handle that?" When Holly nodded again, Joseph raised his voice. "I'm looking for a yes, here!"

"Yes," she said quietly.

"Good! You're learning respect and obedience. Maybe Jared will make a good woman of you yet! Anyway, Simon Banks will be conducting the wedding service, and he's making a special effort to get here a day early—that's tomorrow—so we will be blessed with his Sunday sermon." Holly had been sitting looking at her hands the whole time he was talking, so now he said, "Hey! Are you listening to me or not?"

"I'm listening," said Holly without looking up.

He reached out, grabbed her hand, and gave it a jerk. "I expect you to look at me when I talk to you!"

Holly looked up, stunned by the cruelty in his gray-green eyes. But there was something else there as well—something that made her shiver. And for the first time since she had been in that basement, she noticed the clock over the stairs. It was similar to the hen in the kitchen, but this was a black cat, and as its eyes moved, its tail moved as well. The ticking sound made her feel like it was ticking her life away.

Joseph twisted her wrist until she flinched. "I'm waiting for an answer from you!"

Even though he hadn't asked a question, Holly answered, "Yes."

"That's better!" He released her wrist. "Anyway, you will be attending the Sunday sermon along with everyone else. The church will be packed. And again, I expect you to behave and do whatever Jared tells you to do. Am I understood?"

"Yes." She realized that she could look at the clock directly above his left shoulder, and he would think that she was looking at him.

His gaze softened, and he didn't say anything for a

minute while he examined her face. And when she took her eyes from the clock and looked into his again, she knew exactly what else was in his eyes. Lust. Pure unadulterated lust. She shivered again.

"I'm glad we understand each other then." He stood up and looked at her. "Stand up now." When she hesitated, he reached down, grabbed her wrist and twisted it, hard.

Holly said, "Ouch!" before she could stop herself. He pulled her up and pressed himself against her. With his other hand behind her head, he began to pull her mouth toward his, until they heard the door open upstairs.

"Hey! What's going on down there?" Jared asked.

Joseph released her and said, "Nothing. I was going over the ground rules for tomorrow and Monday. She'll be going to Simon's sermon tomorrow, and she has promised to behave."

Jared walked down the stairs with his head tilted in a funny way. "She did, did she?" he asked when he stepped off the last stair. Then he noticed the look on Holly's face and the marks around her wrist.

Something akin to a thrill went through Holly when she realized where Jared's eyes had gone, so she rubbed her wrist like it still hurt—which actually, it did. Joseph was strong and knew how to use his strength to his advantage.

"Yes, she did," said Joseph, with one foot on the stairs.

"Holly, did he hurt you?" Jared demanded. Before Holly could answer, he said, "No. Don't answer that. Don't give him any more reason to hurt you." He pointed to

Holly's wrist. *"You* did that! And I don't like it! She's *my* woman, and I'd like you to keep your hands *off* her!"

"At least until her first ovo, huh, little brother?" Joseph smiled at Jared and winked at Holly with a lecherous grin on his face.

"Get out of here and leave her alone from now on, or I might change my mind about First Rites!"

The smile slid off Joseph's face. "You wouldn't dare. Not after everything that I've done for you here."

"Just stay away from her, Joseph. Stay away."

"Don't tell me what to do, little brother. I can get rid of her as easily as I got her." Then he stomped up the stairs and slammed the front door when he left.

Jared unexpectedly took Holly tenderly in his arms. "I'm so sorry, Holly, I'm so sorry. It will never happen again. I promise." He lifted her wrist to his mouth and kissed it gently in all the places that were rubbed raw from Joseph's tight grasp. Then he kissed her forehead and her cheeks and her nose with such tenderness that Holly was touched. And when he kissed her lightly on the mouth, and then again, her mouth involuntarily opened to his and she kissed him back. He held her gently but firmly in his arms, and Holly pressed against him as she kissed him. After such a horrible few days, she needed some indication that she was still human. Jared was gentle and sweet, and he had defended her. Maybe it wouldn't be so bad after all being his wife.

CHAPTER EIGHTEEN

BUCK REARDON AND Darryl Alessi climbed into the pickup truck with Darryl driving. Buck opened the plastic bag and pulled out the book. "*There's a Darkness in the Light.* What a load of crap!"

"Crap or not, Carter will want to see it." Darryl shifted the truck into gear and pulled into traffic.

Buck leafed through the book looking for pictures. "What do you think he'll do about it?"

"No telling. He'll probably have to go into seclusion and wait until he gets a revelation on what to do. But I know he won't like it."

"So he'll be really happy that we found it for him, right?" Buck sounded hopeful.

"What do you mean we? You were headed toward the ice cream shop. *I* found it!"

"Ah, come on, Darryl. Let me tell him that *I* found it. Carter doesn't like me."

"Because you don't always do what he says—which I don't understand at all. If you believe he's the Messiah, then why don't you follow exactly what he says so you can get to the Promised Land? When you don't do what he says, you risk going the other direction or getting the strap—or both."

Buck closed the book and put it back into the plastic bag. "Because I *don't* think he's the Messiah, that's why. And if he ever took the strap to me, I'd be outa there."

"What?" Darryl took his eyes off the road and looked at Buck in disbelief. "What do you mean you don't believe he's the Messiah? Then what are you doing here?"

"Darryl, we've been friends since grade school. When you told me that you'd found the Messiah, I thought you were nuts. But when you told me about his revelations"— Buck laughed—"I thought joining up sounded like a good way to get laid!"

Darryl looked at his friend again, signaled, and pulled over to the side of the road. "I should drop you off here and be done with you. I can't believe you, Buck. You're using the religion for your own advantage."

"And you're not, Darryl?"

"It's my *duty* to procreate, and it's how I get to the Promised Land." Darryl gave his head a hard nod and pulled back into traffic.

"Your duty, yeah right. The so-called revelation about the women is the first one you told me about—and you were excited about it. You enjoy your *duty* as much as I do!"

"I enjoy it because I'm giving back to the Light community!" Darryl steered onto the onramp and accelerated.

"I got news for you, buddy. Getting your rocks off for God and country or getting your rocks off 'cause you like how it feels is *exactly* the same. You don't kid me."

Darryl made a noncommittal sound and kept driving. They traveled in silence for several minutes.

When they pulled off the highway at the Plenty, Texas, exit, Buck squirmed in his seat. "So, what do you think? Will you let me say that I found the book?"

"I should tell Carter that you're not really one of us!"

"Oh, come on, Darryl, give me a break. Will you let me say that or not?"

"He might be mad that we stopped for ice cream." Darryl shook his head.

"I'll handle it, I'll handle it. And we do have the fencing in the back of the truck."

"The hardware store isn't anywhere close to the book-store."

"I said that I'd handle it, and I will. Besides, Carter will be so ecstatic that we discovered this book that he'll probably move us up on all the lists! No more sloppy seconds and thirds for us!"

Darryl didn't answer but only nodded his head. When they pulled into the parking lot of the church, he turned to Buck. "Listen, man. Don't screw this up. This place means a lot more to me than just getting laid. I *do* believe Carer is the Messiah, and I'll do whatever he says!"

"Would you drink Kool-Aid for him?" Buck wanted to know.

"That's not fair!"

"Would you or wouldn't you, Darryl? Tell me."

"Well, Carter would never do that. He's not crazy like that other guy."

"Yes or no, Darryl? Would you drink it?"

"If Carter had a revelation that we should drink Kool-Aid, then, yes, I would. I trust him completely."

"Idiot!" Buck said under his breath as he stepped from the truck.

When they walked into Carter's office, Buck handed him the book. "I found this in a bookstore. The author was there giving a reading."

Carter took one look at the book, read the back cover, leafed briefly through it, glanced at the bookmark, and then threw the book across the room with all his might. Buck thought for one terrible moment that maybe he shouldn't have told Carter that he was the one who found the book. But then Carter screamed, "Lies! All of it lies! Why is everybody against me? I'm just trying to do the Lord's work! Gimme back that book!" Buck looked at Darryl, and Darryl picked up the book and handed it back to Carter, who held the book into the air and shook it. "This book—this book—something must be done about this book!" Then he turned and walked into his private sanctuary. Before he closed the door, he turned back to the two men. "I need to meditate right now. Both of you stay here while I contemplate on this." Without another word, he slammed the door to his sanctuary.

Two hours later, Carter emerged with a peaceful look on his face. "I've been given instructions by the Father on what to do about this heretical document. You must get the woman and bring her back to me." He handed Buck a piece of paper. "These are the bookstores where she will be signing books in the next several days." Carter's benevolent smile turned to a snarl. "Get her before she leaves Texas! And don't get caught or mess up!"

The two men nodded and started walking from the room when Carter called them back. "And don't hurt her or *touch* her! She's *mine* to dole out the punishment that she deserves!"

CHAPTER NINETEEN

Could This Be Love?

HOLLY LAY ON the bed thinking about the last few minutes. When she had kissed Jared, he didn't seem surprised.
And when he pulled away to look at her, he said, "I have to
leave now to finish planning our wedding." She had
nodded. He continued, "And I have to lock you in again."

She had smiled and said, "I know. When will you be
back?"

"Soon as I can!" Then he kissed her lightly on the nose,
released her from his arms, climbed the stairs two at a time,
and closed and locked the door.

He was so wonderful and so handsome. His eyes were a
brilliant green with gray flecks in them—similar to
Joseph's, but greener—and without a trace of the cruelty.
And he was such a good kisser! She couldn't remember
when a man had kissed her like that. How long would she
have to lie here, alone, pining for him? The longing she felt

for him was a physical sensation in her stomach that made her fold herself into the fetal position.

All thoughts of escaping and getting away from him and the situation had been replaced by something else. All she could think about was having his warm, protective arms around her again. Being in his arms like that made her feel so safe, so loved. It was a feeling that she wanted more of—a feeling that she wanted to keep forever.

Suddenly she sat up in bed. She didn't even know his last name! Lying back down, she crossed one knee over the other. Mrs. Jared Something. Holly had always thought that she would keep her own name after she got married. But now, she wanted everything of his—his name, his lips, his kisses, his arms around her. She wanted to be possessed by the feeling of safety that he offered. And with that thought, she closed her eyes, and fell asleep with the taste of him still fresh on her lips.

Sometime later—she was too disoriented from falling asleep in the middle of the day to know how long—she heard Jared's voice at the top of the stairs. "Honey! I'm home!"

Jumping out of bed, she ran from the room and up the stairs with an urgency she couldn't contain. He stood there in the kitchen, drinking a glass of water. The look on his face as she flew into his arms surprised her. How could he not know how she felt? She pressed herself into him and held up her head to kiss him once again.

But he took her by the shoulders and pushed her gently

away. "No. I can't kiss you anymore. We just have to wait." He must have noticed the hurt in her eyes, because he kissed her on the forehead. "Holly, we're getting married in two days. And I know you want to please me. But as much as I want to make love to you right now, I would rather wait and have our wedding night be special. Because *you're* special. So no more kissing until then, okay?"

She snuggled back into him. "We can still cuddle, though?"

He pushed her away to arm's length. "Not like *that*, we can't!" Lifting her chin with his fingers, he said, "Come on, Holly. It's only two days! A day and a half, really. We can wait, right?"

Stepping backwards, she smiled at him and raised her eyebrows. "Tell me about our wedding!"

"I can't, silly girl! It's supposed to be a surprise! And it's all handled. Susan just has to work out the details, but she's good at that, so I'm not concerned. I'm very grateful that Simon consented to come out and marry us. You'll like him. He's an extraordinary person, and I can't wait for him to meet you."

"You hungry, Jared? Because I'm starved." She opened the refrigerator and then turned back to him. "And I'm *cooking*!"

"Then yes! I was definitely getting tired of eating TV dinners every night!"

Holly pulled the package of chicken out of the refrigerator, put it on the counter, then looked at him from over her shoulder. "That's what wives are for! Cooking dinner!" Reaching over to the oven, she turned it on to 350 degrees.

"I'll be right back, I—"

She looked at him when he hesitated. The smile was off his face, and he looked disturbed.

"What is it, Jared? What's wrong?" She dropped the chicken on the counter and stepped up to him, looking into his beautiful eyes.

"I need to use the restroom. You—you aren't going to run away on me, are you?"

She took his hands. How could he not know how much she loved him? Didn't it show in her eyes? "Jared, I'm not going anywhere. I *love* you."

"Oh, Holly!" He put his arms around her and held her tight. "I love you, too. I love you *so* much!" And despite his previous words, he pulled her into him and kissed her passionately. Then, just as quickly, he moved her to arm's length again. "I'll be right back."

"And I'll have the chicken in the oven before you get back!"

But she didn't. Although he took longer than she expected, it wasn't long enough to find everything that she needed. Susan had shown her where most of the food was—before Joseph had stormed in—but Holly had no idea where any of the pots and pans were. In her searching, she had opened one drawer that had an ovo test kit in it, but she didn't pay it any mind. Dinner was the only thing on her mind, so she passed it by, and continued looking for pots and pans.

"What are you looking for?" asked Jared, his voice stiff with concern.

"Your pots and pans! I told you I'd have the chicken in the oven, but I can't find anything to put it in!"

"Oh," said Jared, sounding relieved. "I don't have much. Right here." He opened a cabinet and pulled out one Dutch oven, a saucepan with a lid, and a frying pan.

"That's it?" asked Holly, taking the three items from him. "I need more than that if I'm going to cook you dinner every night!"

He smiled at her and winked. "Well, we will be getting wedding gifts!"

"The wedding! Gifts! Awesome!" she said and put the chicken into the Dutch oven. While she worked, he stood in the kitchen and talked to her the whole time, telling her about his day, about the different people who had stopped by the gas station, and completely leaving out any mention of the wedding. But it was okay. She didn't mind him leaving that out because she liked that he wanted to surprise her. And she loved hearing about his day. It made her feel complete in a way that she'd never known.

As they sat down to eat, Jared began telling her about what Simon's sermon would be like. Although he made it sound interesting, it in no way prepared her for what she was about to experience the following day.

CHAPTER TWENTY

Sunday Sermon

After Jared unlocked her from the basement in the morning, Holly cooked them breakfast. But it took too long, so they left late for church and had to park Jared's big truck on the street and walk two blocks. Holly's first impression of the church was that it was *huge*. Huge and painted gold. Jared, carrying something white in his hand, explained to her that it had to be huge, because everyone in the town of Plenty was a member of the Children of the Light, and they all attended church. She just nodded, intimidated by the size of the place.

When he opened the gold door for her to enter, she noticed all the stained glass windows depicting biblical scenes. Then he opened the interior door of the church, and Holly was shocked to see all the women and children seated in the back and the men seated up front.

"This is where I leave you," Jared whispered, though

the service hadn't quite begun. "Go ahead and sit there, with Marina and Susan."

Holly looked where Jared pointed to see Marina patting the seat beside her. She turned to say good-bye to him, but he had already walked off. When she looked again at the men in the front of the church, she realized that they all wore white robes. That must have been what Jared had in his hand, because when she looked to see where he had disappeared to, he had been lost in a sea of white.

"Sit here, quickly!" said Marina. "If Simon's in a bad mood, he's been known to throw women out if they're restless or not seated when he begins."

"What if a *man* is restless?" Holly whispered back.

Marina shrugged and then the service began. "That's Simon on stage now," she whispered.

Holly looked forward and saw Simon walk onto the stage. Although the stage was far away from her, she could see him perfectly because of the two large viewing screens behind him. They made him larger than life. And if those huge screens weren't enough, there were four more that had unrolled on the sides of the church by the time he reached center stage.

Simon was a tall man in his mid-fifties dressed in white like the rest of the men. He had dark hair and piercingly dark eyes that Holly felt looked right through her. It made her feel uncomfortable in a way, but it also fascinated her. Before he even spoke a word and even at this distance, she could feel that charisma radiated out of him like a bright sun. His movements were sensual, so when Marina leaned over and whispered quietly in her ear, "I wish *he* was available for my first ovo," Holly understood exactly what she meant. Women would fall for a man like this, and be more than willing to do as he asked. When she felt the stirrings of desire begin in her, she immediately pushed them away. She didn't like men like that, and she especially didn't like the way they made her—and every other woman—feel. His very being reminded her of Charles Manson or Jim Jones.

Simon raised his arms, looked skyward, and said, "I am the Light!"

The whole congregation chanted in unison, "You are Thee Light."

Then Simon brought his arms down and held them out toward the congregation. "You are the Light."

The congregation chanted, "We are the Light."

"*I*"—pause—"am the Messiah, and *you*"—pause—"are the power and likeness of God."

He pointed to himself and then back again to the audience, but he must have meant only the men, because when Holly started to repeat his words, Marina elbowed her hard in the ribs. "Simon could have you thrown out for that!" she scowled.

When the usually cheerful Marina reacted like that, Holly looked up quickly to see if Simon had noticed her blunder. But he stood there in silence with his hands folded in front of his chest and his head bowed. Then he began to speak again.

"Women"—pause—"are blessings in our life, to be sure. But we must remember that they are chattel, and we should treat them as such. Yes"—pause—"they are the ones who bear our children, but *we*"—pause—"are the ones who *give* them those children. They could not have children without *us*. That is why God made *men* in his image, because *we* are the chosen ones.

"Still, we need to respect and cherish our women for the service they do for *us* and for our God. At the same time, we will not tolerate disobedience. Just as a man should not beat a dog just for being a dog, a man should not beat his wife just because he can. But if that dog chews up his slippers, the dog must be punished so it won't do it again—or do something worse. In the same way, if a wife is disobedient, she must be punished as well. Only *you*"—pause—"each of *you*"—pause—"know how severe that punishment might need to be, because only *you*"—pause—"know your own women.

"I encourage you all not to be abusive, but I also counsel you very strongly, not to let them get away with *anything*. They are beautiful, but they are not as smart as us, and they need our guidance. If they think they can get one over on you, they will, and it will only work out badly for everyone. So I beseech you, keep your women in line!"

Simon looked out at the men in his audience, and it was like he was making eye contact with each of them. All the men watched Simon and nodded their heads up and down. She could hear a few murmurs of "Yes!" from the men seated in the front section of the church. A few minutes later, the tone of the sermon changed. It was palpable, and she could feel the tension lifting from the room. The entire time the speech had been going on, not one woman uttered one word.

"That reminds me of a joke," Simon said. He told a joke about a priest and a rabbi, and the punch line was about women getting raped. The men roared with laughter, and the women—surprisingly enough—also broke into laughter.

Holly looked around the room, mortified. This Simon, as charismatic as he was, was in every way a misogynist. She didn't listen to anything else the man said, and she began to wonder about Jared's involvement with this whole group. It gave her a bad feeling in her stomach, but then she remembered about some friends from college who had married. Jill was Catholic and Jim was Jewish. They got married, had children, were happy and still married last she had heard. So even if Holly didn't buy into all this weird Children of the Light rhetoric, she and Jared could still be happy together. Couldn't they?

Suddenly, a loud sound disrupted Holly's thoughts, and she saw movement all around her. All the women in the room, including Marina and Susan, had stood up. Holly stood up and discovered where the sound had come from. Two large movable doors, from floor to ceiling, were sliding across the room several rows in front of her. Judging by the sound of their movement, they were heavy and soundproof. While Holly watched in amazement, Marina bumped into her from behind.

"Follow the other women out, Holly."

Holly stood by the aisle until there was a break in the stream of women. The doors had sealed shut by then, and were, indeed, soundproof. Although Simon had spoken loudly using a microphone, she could still hear the rise and fall of his voice, but she couldn't make out a single word. If he freely spilled that misogynist rhetoric with the women still in the room, she wondered what he would talk about with the women gone.

When they had walked into the large entryway, she found the other women setting up tables and placing different kinds of food and drink on them. After Susan introduced her to several women, Holly asked Marina what Simon could possibly be telling the men.

"Secret stuff," said Marina. "It's none of our business."

"What if it's about us?" asked Holly.

Marina shrugged. "Still none of our business."

"Would Susan know, or who else can I ask?"

Susan had overheard this part of the conversation, so she turned around. "Holly, I don't know and neither do any of the other women. And I would advise you not to ask anyone. There is no place for questions in our society here. Asking them can only get you into trouble. What the men want you to know, they'll tell you. Everything else is better left unknown." She seemed about to say something else, but then the doors opened, and the men—still dressed in white and looking like hoodless Ku Klux Klansmen—started pouring into the room. "Here, Holly. Have some cheese and keep quiet. Here comes Simon."

Joseph reached her first, followed by Simon with Jared coming up from behind. "And here, Simon, is the woman that Jared will marry tomorrow. Simon, this is Holly. Say hello to Simon, Holly." He nodded with a stern expression on his face as if he expected her to refuse.

Holly nodded her head, smiled, and said, "Very nice meeting you, Simon."

Simon's eyes widened when he saw her. He took her hand, held it up to his lips, and kissed it gently. "And *very* nice meeting you, my dear." He looked her up and down and smiled. "I wish I were staying in town longer so we could get better acquainted." Raising his eyebrows, he winked at her, and then walked over to the punch bowl, followed by Joseph.

Jared had gotten distracted talking to someone else, so Holly could hear quite clearly when Simon, who was still leering at her, leaned forward to Joseph, "So when is her ovo? She'd almost be worth staying in town for."

CHAPTER TWENTY-ONE

They Call Them Appointments

HOLLY WENT PALE when she heard Simon's words. It did more than disgust her, it sickened her. The man was an old lech, and she wanted to get away from him. When Jared walked up to her a minute later, she whispered, "Can we please go home now?"

"Oh, sure." He turned to look for Susan and Marina, but they were right there beside Holly. "You ready to go, girls? Joseph has to take Simon to an appointment, so you're coming home with us."

"Sure, we're ready," said Susan.

"I was hoping to talk to Simon," said Marina.

"Another time, Marina. He's leaving right now." Jared turned to walk away. "Come on, everybody."

Holly watched Marina turn and frown as she saw Joseph and Simon walk out the side door of the church. Following Jared, Susan, and Marina out the door, Holly finally breathed easier. She didn't even want to be in the same — large — room with Simon, and having him officiate at the wedding between her and Jared made her feel sick to her stomach. There was nothing to be done about it now though. It was already arranged, and tomorrow was the wedding.

Susan and Marina climbed into the backseat of the truck, and Holly climbed into the front. Although she felt disturbed from Simon's unwanted attention, just being around Jared calmed her. During the drive home, Jared rambled on about how great the sermon was today, while Susan, Marina, and Holly kept silent. When they walked into the house, and Susan and Marina sat down in the living room, Holly pulled Jared aside.

"Jared, does Simon have to be the one to marry us?"

"Holly, yes. He came all the way out here just to perform the ceremony. It's a great honor that he did that. You should feel proud."

"I don't."

He draped an arm around her and walked her into the living room. "You're just having pre-wedding jitters. You'll be fine tomorrow."

Feeling vulnerable thinking of Simon at their wedding after what he had said in front of her, she turned suddenly and wrapped her arms around Jared. "Hold me for a minute, Jared. I just need to feel safe." She didn't notice that Susan and Marina were both surprised at the show of affection.

"Come on, let's sit down." Jared led her to the couch and sat down, pulling her down beside him. She slipped off her shoes, curled her legs under her, and snuggled into him, with her head on his shoulder. "So what did you think of the sermon today, Holly? It was good, wasn't it?"

"I thought it was"—movement across the room attracted Holly's attention. It was Susan, slowly almost imperceptibly, shaking her head from side to side—"um, interesting."

"What did you think?" Jared asked, nodding toward Susan and Marina.

"It was great," said Susan.

"I just *love* Simon!" said Marina.

Then the three of them discussed the finer points of the sermon—including the rape joke that they all found oh-so-funny—while Holly stayed silent with her eyes closed and her head buried in Jared's chest. Thirty minutes later, Jared unwrapped himself from Holly and stood up.

"I have an appointment to go to. I'll be back in an hour or so." He kissed Holly on the lips. "See you all later. When I get back, I'll take you two home." Nodding and smiling, he walked out the front door.

"Holly! Something's changed!" Marina leaned forward in her chair to look at Holly.

Holly shrugged and shook her head. "Nothing's changed."

"You *like* Jared! For real! You're not pretending! I could see it in your eyes!"

"Yeah, I do like him. He's kind to me. So what?"

"You know where he's going now, right?" asked Susan.

"To an appointment." Holly looked at her blankly.

Marina giggled. Susan said simply, "That's what they call it."

Puzzled, Holly looked at Susan and Marina and said, "What do you mean?"

"He's procreating, Holly!" Marina burst out, still giggling.

Susan nodded, frowned, and raised her eyebrows. Holly shook her head, not believing. "No, he's not! You're just saying that."

"That's exactly where he is, Holly! And the reason he brought us over here is because Joseph took Simon over there, and when they finish, then it's Jared's turn."

Holly huffed through her nose. "Well, we're not married yet. He won't do it *after* we're married."

"He *has* to! It's how men get to the Promised Land!" shouted Marina, while Susan nodded. "Besides, if he doesn't, then Joseph will punish him."

Holly set her jaw and shook her head. "I know he'll find a way."

"There's something else you should know," said Susan. "Jared is going to ask you to take an ovo test soon."

"No. First Rites. I'll never have to do that ten-men thing."

"Yes, you will. Joseph has already made up a list of nine other men for you. And I have to tell you, Holly, that they're the worst men in town."

"Not that it matters, but what do you mean they're the worst men?"

"The *mean* ones. The ones that will knock you around before they take you. I recognized the names." Susan shrugged. "I'm sorry, Holly, but I thought you should know."

"It doesn't matter. Jared told Joseph he would claim First Rites."

"No, he didn't. The reason that Joseph arrested you— for Jared—to begin with is because Jared told him that he *wouldn't* claim First Rites. Jared may have threatened later that he was *going* to claim them, but he won't. He had already given his word to Joseph, and he won't go back on it. Trust me, he won't."

"I don't know why you're telling me this, Susan, and I don't believe you. Jared wouldn't do that to me. I know he wouldn't."

Marina stood up, walked across the room, sat down next to Holly, put her arm around her, and said to Susan, "It's okay, Susan. If she doesn't believe you now, she will later. Let it go for now." Then she turned to Holly. "Let's talk about how great your wedding is going to be tomorrow, because I know it's going to be super! Wait till you see how they decorate the church!"

"I know it's going to be perfect," said Holly. "Really perfect."

CHAPTER TWENTY-TWO

Not Quite Crawling Down the Aisle

HOLLY AWOKE THE following morning, still locked in the basement, but with a smile on her face. She was getting married today to the man of her dreams. Jared was handsome, kind, and affectionate. Although Susan's words came back to her, she pushed them away. Things would change once they were married. She knew they would. And Jared would claim First Rites, as long as she got pregnant right away—a light went off in her brain, but she couldn't figure out why. Brushing it aside, she continued smiling while she got dressed.

When she heard the bolt sliding open from above, she ran to the bottom of the stairs to see Jared. Her shoulders and smile drooped when she saw that it was Susan with Marina behind her. They both wore dresses and looked more dressed up than usual. The dresses were still muted colors, with Marina in beige and Susan in brown.

"Where's Jared?"

"Holly, you know you can't see him before the wedding. Marina and I brought you breakfast." She walked slowly downstairs carrying donuts, coffee, and orange juice.

"Oh, no! Don't tell me we're back to donuts! Can't I go upstairs and make oatmeal or something?"

"Jared's still up there. You have to stay down here. I'll help you with the donuts!" Marina sat down at the table.

Holly sat down across from Marina, reluctantly took a donut out of the box, and kept glancing upstairs, as if she expected Jared to appear. She took a sip of the coffee, and said, "Oh! Thank you for bringing me breakfast, Susan. I do appreciate it. Honest, I do."

"You're getting married today, Holly! Are you still excited?" asked Marina.

"Yes, I'm a little nervous, though." She looked at Susan. "You helped him plan the wedding, right? So you know exactly what's going to happen?" Susan nodded. "He's not going to make me crawl down the aisle, is he?"

Marina laughed. "No! The only person who ever did that was Joseph!"

Susan nodded. "She's right. Joseph did that to me because he was angry."

"Angry at what?" asked Holly.

Susan looked down and played with the sprinkles that had fallen off her donut. Then she exhaled long and slow and shook her head from side to side.

"If you don't want to say, it's okay," said Holly.

Susan nodded and began. "I was in love with Derek Sanderson. And he was in love with me. We had planned to be married, but Joseph wanted me, and he somehow got Simon to refuse to sanction the marriage between Derek and me. So I was supposed to marry Joseph on Sunday. And back then—it was before the whole ovo thing—I was still a virgin, which of course was why Joseph wanted me all the more. But I hated that he had separated me from the man I loved, so the night before the wedding, I slept with Derek. Joseph found out. So the following day, at our wedding, he forced me to crawl all the way down the aisle. What a spectacle I made!" She shook her head and exhaled again.

"Tell her the rest, Susan. She should know," said Marina.

"I got pregnant right away, and Joseph insisted that it was Derek's—and frankly, I think he was right. So he hit me and hit me, in the face and even more in the stomach, until I started hemorrhaging. I was rushed to the hospital where they performed an emergency hysterectomy—so I can never have children."

"So now, the only way she can get to the Promised Land is by obeying Joseph," said Marina.

Holly looked at Susan after nodding to Marina. "Susan, there are other ways into Heaven."

Susan nodded. "I know. Marina told me everything you told her. I've been thinking about that."

Holly turned her head and looked at Susan. "So—if you

had a hysterectomy and don't ovulate, then you don't have to do the procreation thing, right?"

Susan laughed, but not as if she were amused. "At first, I didn't. Then Joseph found out that I didn't like the procreating, so he insisted that I participate. He made up a date—third of the month, because that was the date that I lost my virginity to Derek—and now every third and fourth, I have ten men visit me each day."

Holly shook her head. "Oh, man, Susan. I'm sorry."

"Oh, it's not as bad as it was. At first, Joseph would assign the worst men in town—the ones that he's assigned to you now. But then, he got easier with me and left out the mean ones."

"What happened to Derek Sanderson?" asked Holly.

The basement door opened and Joseph's voice boomed down the stairs. "Jared left. You have ten minutes to get her dressed so we can get out of here."

"Come on," said Susan. "Let's get you dressed and married!"

"I get dressed here?" asked Holly.

"It's done differently here. Come on, let me help you get your dress on, and you'll see." Susan led the way into Holly's bedroom.

Marina jumped up, pulled Holly back a little to separate them from Susan, and she whispered, "I've heard rumors that Joseph had Derek murdered. He was never seen or heard from again." Stunned, Holly swallowed, shook her head to get the dark thoughts out of it, and followed Susan into the bedroom.

When they walked out to Joseph's truck ten minutes later, Holly was dressed in her black wedding dress and her black shoes. Susan had brushed her hair until it had a bright sheen to it and tied it back in a tight bun. As Holly looked in the mirror, she thought she looked beautiful. And she was getting married today!

"Here, Holly, you can sit in the front with Joseph, since you're the guest of honor," said Susan.

"I don't want her up here with me," grumbled Joseph. "She can sit in the back with chatterbox."

Susan shrugged and opened the back door for Holly, then closed it behind her. She climbed into the truck, and Joseph backed the truck out of the driveway without another word.

Holly was uncomfortable around Joseph and kept silent. So did Susan and Marina. A few minutes passed, and they were in front of the church. The parking lot was full and so was the street. It looked like everyone in town was there.

"Wow, it's crowded. Where will you park?" asked Holly.

"He's the sheriff. He can do anything he wants," said Marina. "And he usually does."

"Shut up, Marina. Get out of the car, Holly, I'm not waiting here all day."

Holly tried the door, but it wouldn't open. "Oh, sorry, Holly. I have to open mine first." Susan opened her door and then opened Holly's. "I'll see you in a minute! Walk slow, and don't be scared!"

Holly stepped out and timidly looked at Susan and then at Marina. She *was* scared. She didn't know what to do or what to expect. Susan started closing the door, but Marina scooted over in the seat and said, "Wait! Holly, there's something we forgot to tell you! You have to get down on your hands and knees for the vows!"

CHAPTER TWENTY-THREE

DEAN WAS THRILLED when they finally drove away from Texas. Five days, five cities, ending with Austin, and now they were done. He had been on alert ever since he had seen the two men and had never let Olivia go anywhere without him. Much to Olivia's dismay and sometimes embarrassment, he even checked the restrooms before he allowed her to go in. She put up a fuss, but he wasn't going to let anything happen to her, even if she never spoke to him again. Besides, Dean thought that she secretly liked him doting on her like that.

The two men never showed up at any of the other cities —that he knew of—although he thought he had seen a couple of men in the same pickup parked outside more than one bookstore. It was a plain white pickup, though, just like dozens of others that he had seen since coming to Texas, and it had tinted windows, so he couldn't see the men inside.

"Now that we're leaving Texas, you must be disappointed that you can't look after me anymore." Olivia used the mirror on her visor to retouch her makeup.

Dean glanced at her and then back at the road. "I know

you're going to fight me on this, Olivia, and I know that you've said you're not ready, but I'm moving in with you—temporarily—just in case." He glanced at her again and saw that her mouth was open. "Temporarily."

"Dean, that's not necessary, and I don't want you to. I like my own space. You know that."

"I know that, Olivia. And I like you alive, and I'm going to make sure that you stay that way."

"You're making much too much of this. You never saw those men again. They probably just stumbled onto the bookstore and were interested in my book—like everyone else. That's not so hard to believe, is it?"

"I have no doubt in my mind that those men were from the cult. And from the bookstore, they went directly back to Weeks to give him the book."

"You mean de la Luz."

Dean waved his hand in the air. "Whatever."

"Then maybe he didn't care. It is fiction, after all." Olivia put a dab of powder on her nose, snapped shut her case, and flipped the visor back up.

"Olivia, it will only be two or three weeks. I just want to make sure you're safe—and I want to get you a gun."

"Absolutely not! I will not have a gun in my house!"

"Come off it, Olivia. You have a gun in your house every time I stay over."

"Yeah, well, that's different. It's *your* gun."

"Okay, fine. This will be my gun, too, but it will be in your house where you can get it if you need it."

"Dean, really, what are the chances that they are going to come to my house? Be realistic!"

"I *am* being realistic, Olivia! *You're* not! They've already killed people. Other people have disappeared. Why not you? And don't tell me because you're a best-selling author, because they don't care about that."

"Honestly, Dean." Olivia made a soft snort through her nose and looked out the side window.

"And I want you to remember how I described those two men. One of them had on a Dallas Cowboys' cap, and the other had on a John Deere cap. The Cowboys' guy was big and muscular; the John Deere guy was tall and thin."

"And what if they've changed their hats—?" Another snort through her nose.

"Just watch out for them, okay?"

"Mmmmm."

"I think maybe I should take some more time off—at least for the next few days."

She turned toward him with narrowed eyes. "No way, Dean. I need my space! You've been hovering over me and following me around like a puppy dog. At least give me a day off!"

"But I'm supposed to work a double shift tomorrow. I'll see if I can change it and just work one."

"No! Give me some space! I love you, but you're carrying this whole protecting me thing too far. There's nothing that I need to be protected from! I'm safe! Leave a gun with me if it will make you feel better, but you need to back off a little."

"I can sleep in the guest room, then."

"Oh, Dean." She put her hand on his arm and rubbed it. "No, I don't want you in the guest room. I want you with me, but I need you to let me be by myself for a while. Go to work.

Stay both shifts. I'll be fine."

"I'm thinking maybe of getting you a Rottweiler for when I'm not there."

"Sorry, Dean. I'd rather have the gun. Guns don't leave dog hairs on the carpet or furniture."

For the rest of the trip, there was just small talk or silence. Dean was trying to give her the space she needed and with the two of them in the car, silence was the only way he could do that.

When they drove into town, instead of going straight to Olivia's house, Dean drove to his house, picked up a gun, and then drove to Olivia's. He made her wait in the car—holding the gun—while he inspected her house carefully before she entered. Then he carried the bags inside while she walked in front of him. Nothing was going to happen to Olivia on his watch. And it was always his watch.

CHAPTER TWENTY-FOUR

A Cultish Wedding

HOLLY WATCHED AS the truck sped off after squealing its wheels. She sighed and thought that until she reached the end of the aisle, she would be all alone in the world. But when she got there, she'd be with Jared, her dream man. She turned around, and it wasn't until then that she noticed all the flower petals on the sidewalk before her.

Alternate red and white rose petals lined each side of the walkway leading to the church. Oh, Jared, she thought, what a romantic you are! Slowly, she made her way up the sidewalk toward the doors of the church. When she got close enough to open them, they opened by themselves and two men dressed in white smiled at her and motioned with their arms showing her the way.

Inside the church, the lines of alternating red and white rose petals still showed her the way, but once inside the inner church doors, there was a profusion of red and white rose petals on her path where she walked. It was so absolutely beautiful that tears came to her eyes, and she tried to blink them away. Then she looked up, and there was Jared at the end of the aisle, smiling warmly at her. Dressed all in white—as were the men who had opened the church doors for her—he looked like the handsomest man on earth. Although her attention remained focused on Jared, she noticed that women and children were not confined to the back of the church this time, and the large screens—both in the front and on the sides—were not lowered.

As she approached the altar, Jared put out his hand to her, beckoning her to him. It was then that she saw Simon standing behind Jared. He had a big grin on his face and looked at her with leering eyes. But incredibly, she still felt his charisma reaching out to her, and as much as he disgusted her, she felt drawn to him.

Holly walked up the ramp to the stage and took Jared's hand. Simon didn't matter anymore. Nobody did. Only Jared. He took both of her hands in his and gazed into her eyes with love and wonder. And she gazed back into his, giving him her whole heart.

"Friends, we are gathered here today to establish the permanent ownership of this woman by this man," began Simon. Holly winced at ownership, but neither Jared nor Simon noticed it. "We all understand," continued Simon, "that ownership of a woman is not unlike ownership of a dog or a car. And yet, there are differences. We must honor and comfort the woman, and protect and provide for her.

Are you willing to do that, Jared Tanner?"

Jared smiled and squeezed Holly's hands. "Yes, Simon, I definitely am."

"It is also the man's responsibility to punish the woman if she is not obedient or if she strays beyond the bounds of conventional behavior. Are you willing to do that, Jared Tanner?"

"Yes, Simon, I am," said Jared, still smiling into her eyes. Then he nodded to her and released her hands.

"Now it is time for your vows, Holly O'Neill." Simon hesitated and looked at her, nodding his head in an exaggerated manner. She started hearing whispers in the audience, and then Holly remembered what Marina had told her.

"Oh!" Holly said under her breath and got down on her hands and knees. Simon didn't speak and the audience continued to whisper.

Marina, whom Holly hadn't noticed was in the front row sitting with Susan and Joseph, whispered loudly, "Put your head on his shoes!"

Holly looked up, thinking that Marina was kidding, but the girl had a serious expression on her face and was nodding. So Holly leaned farther down and rested her head on Jared's shiny, black shoes.

"Holly O'Neill," started Simon, "as this man's possession, do you promise to love and honor him as your Lord and master?"

Holly didn't know if she should answer or not, but when she heard whispers from the audience, she said, "Yes" while hoping that she wasn't supposed to pick up her head when she said it. When the ceremony didn't continue, Holly said it louder, "Yes!"

"And, as this man's possession, do you promise to obey him at all costs and do whatever he deems necessary?"

It was only when Simon repeated the phrase "as this man's possession" that Holly really heard it. The first time he said it, she was still getting used to being in a kneeling position in front of the whole congregation and having her head on Jared's shoes. Possession? She didn't like that, and she didn't like the "obey" part either. But that must be how they word it here, so she said, "Yes!" as loudly as she could, so they could hear her.

"Traditionally, now is the time that I ask the bride to stand up and I complete the ceremony. But since you are new to our church here, Holly, we need to do one more small thing before you stand up. All right?"

"Yes!" said Holly. She was uncomfortable and just wanted to get this over with—not just to stand up, but to begin her life with Jared.

"Do you, Holly O'Neill, willingly join the flock of the Children of the Light, accept all the tenets of this church, and do you promise to obey them and *me* with all your heart?"

Obey *him*, wondered Holly. She didn't sign up for this. It was one thing marrying Jared and having him be a part of this crazy religion, but she had to be too? Obey Simon? That charismatic, lecherous old goat? Gross!

"And do you promise to accept me as the one and only Messiah, the Prince of Peace, and the Light of the World?" Simon continued.

As Holly hesitated, this time there wasn't a sound in the entire church. Well, she thought, she had already come this far and promised to be Jared's possession, she might as well go all the way. "Yes, I do," she said. She felt like the entire audience gave a collective sigh.

"Stand up, my dear," said Simon.

Holly stood up, and Jared took her hands again. "Jared, do you have the wedding bracelet?"

"Oh!" said Jared and stuck his hand in his pants pocket, pulling out a golden bracelet with a small open lock hanging off one end. Holly, not knowing what else to do, held out her right wrist. "The other one, Holly," Jared said.

"Put the bracelet on her wrist, Jared." Simon waited until Jared put the bracelet on. "Now close the lock to symbolize your ownership and her servitude to you and you alone."

Jared snapped the lock closed, while Holly watched and listened with disbelief. It was the way they did things around here, she kept telling herself. She hated that these little weirdnesses were distracting her from what could have been a lovely ceremony. Glancing at the aisle she had walked down—the rose petals that she had walked on— made her smile again and look at Jared.

"I now pronounce you man and wife," said Simon. "You can kiss the bride!"

Jared leaned forward to kiss her, while the audience erupted with applause. Then Joseph stepped up to shake Jared's hand, while Simon turned Holly around to face him.

"And now, *I* kiss the bride," he said, while he plastered his mouth to Holly's and slid his tongue between her lips.

CHAPTER TWENTY-FIVE

THE MORE MILES Buck drove, the madder he got. He tightened his hands on the steering wheel until his knuckles turned white. His teeth were clenched, and he was doing his best to hold in his anger. With one hand, he released the steering wheel and hit the dashboard as hard as he could.

"What's up with you, dude?" Darryl looked at him in surprise.

"I hate the way Carter treats us!" Buck growled.

Darryl shrugged. "He's the Messiah. He can treat us any way he likes. And we have to take it if we're going to the Promised Land."

"Do you really believe that garbage, Darryl?"

"Yes, of course I do. Everything I do, I do for him."

"Idiot," Buck said under his breath. "I only wish he had said to kill the woman! I would have liked to do that—and pretend it was Carter that I was killing."

Darryl sat up in the seat. "Now you've gone too far, Buck. You can't talk about him that way! I won't stand for it! I don't care how long we've been friends!"

Buck glanced over at Darryl and scowled. "Fine. I wish I'd

never agreed to this. I'll do it, though, because it might be exciting kidnapping someone. But once we get back and deliver our *prey* to him, I'm done. I'll miss getting laid all the time, but the rest of the crap isn't worth it for me."

Darryl stayed silent and then said softly, "You know, Buck, Carter had a reason to yell at us like that. We didn't bring him the woman like he asked."

"Darryl, was there any possible way to get that woman without shooting the guy who was with her every second of every day? No, of course not! It was impossible. He shouldn't have treated us that way."

Darryl didn't say anything more, and neither did Buck. Hours passed and scenery went by and neither man said a word. Finally, when they drove past the sign that said "Entering Arizona," Darryl spoke. "What if that guy is still guarding her all the time?"

"He won't be. He'll feel safe now that they're out of Texas and back home."

"Yeah, but what if he is? I don't like getting yelled at by Carter any more than you do."

Buck reached into the overnight bag beside him. Although they had planned to drive straight through, Buck brought this with him. He reached in and pulled out a gun, waving it in the air. "If he is, I'll take care of him! Without a public place to worry about, I'll just take him right out of the picture." He gave a little chuckle.

"Put that away, Buck! What are you doing? We don't want to be stopped by the cops!"

Buck put the gun back in the bag. "No worries, Darryl. Arizona is an open-carry state. Every redneck in the state has a gun."

Darryl hunkered down in the seat and pulled the green John Deere hat over his eyes, which made Buck chuckle again. He adjusted his own blue Cowboys hat and settled into his seat. Wondering why he suddenly felt better, he realized that he always felt better with a gun in his hand. And the possibility to use it? Awesome! Who knew what excitement the future hours could bring. Kidnap a woman? Check. Kill her boyfriend if he got in the way? Check. Have his way with the woman before they returned to Plenty? Check. No more of that seconds and thirds and fourths for him. This time he'd be first and enjoy every minute of it! And if Carter gave him any trouble, he'd put a bullet in him, too. Messiah, my ass, thought Buck.

He began to whistle softly through his teeth and sway to a rhythm only he could hear. Nodding his head, he thought about what he would do after they returned the woman to Carter. There was no way he would stay any longer at the cult—that's all that it was. Darryl may be stupid enough to drink Kool-Aid for that weirdo Carter, but he wasn't. Buck had months of getting laid every day, but he worked essentially for free, and now he needed to make some money, which he couldn't do at the cult. If he had some money, he could afford prostitutes, or maybe even take a nice girl out and get lucky. If he had money, he could do anything. And he would.

When he thought they were getting close, Buck reached over and whacked Darryl on the leg. "Wake up, little buddy, and give me directions on how to get to her house. Hey, how did Carter find out where she lived anyway? He must have a private line to God or something!" He laughed at his own joke while Darryl fiddled with the map.

"Good thing I woke up. Get off at the next exit, turn right, and drive five miles. When the road splits, immediately take the first right. Twenty-four ten. Big white house. Hedges in front to hide the truck."

"Big white house? Hedges? How *does* he know that?"

Darryl flipped his hand in the air. "Whatever."

As they approached the address, Buck slowed the truck down, turned into the driveway, and parked. A red BMW was parked in the driveway, but the white truck they had seen the man drive in Texas was nowhere to be found. Shucks, thought Buck. No killin' today. Looking at his watch, he saw that it was noon. Maybe if they hung around for a while, they could catch him coming home from work. Naw, just get her and get out. Darryl would complain anyway, he thought.

After turning off the engine, he reached back into the bag, took out the gun, and stuck it in the back of his pants. When Darryl saw that, he said, "Hey. The guy's truck isn't here. You won't need that."

"Security, Darryl. What if she puts up a fight?" He grabbed a sock out of the bag and handed it to Darryl. "We'll need this, too. You carry it." Then he stepped out of the truck and instead of closing the door, he opened the back door and left them both open.

The two men walked up to the house and knocked on the door.

CHAPTER TWENTY-SIX

At the Reception

SHOCKED AT THE unwanted kiss she received from Simon, Holly pulled away from him, and he drew back his hand and slapped her hard across the face. "Don't *ever* pull away from me again. *Nobody* pulls away from *me*." Then he shoved her away from him.

Holly looked out at the audience, but everyone was milling around or congratulating Jared. No one had noticed. Then she saw Susan and Marina standing almost in front of her. Susan had a grim expression on her face, and Marina was blinking back tears.

Susan grasped Holly's arm and tucked it under her own. "Come on, let's get you to the reception line."

Holly, still recovering not only from Simon's slap but from the ceremony itself, asked, "Shouldn't I walk up with Jared?"

"No, he's already walked up with the men. You go with

us."

Holly looked behind her and saw that Jared had indeed left without her. She shook her head and clenched her jaw. This wedding wasn't anything like she had imagined it would be.

Marina came to the other side of Holly and said, "I'm so sorry, Holly. It's my fault. I should have told you that Simon would kiss you after the ceremony." She wiped tears from her eyes. "But I can't believe that he slapped you! In front of all those people! It was horrible!"

Holly, her breath ragged and on the verge of tears herself, said, "I don't think anyone noticed, really. It's okay, Marina. It's not your fault."

"After what he did to you, I don't want to lose my virginity to him after all! I *hate* him!"

"Shhh," said Susan. "Be quiet or you'll get yourself excommunicated."

"Susan," Holly said quietly so no one else could hear, "did you know he was going to—I don't know what to call it—convert me up there?"

Susan shook her head. "No, he's never done that before, but you're the first outsider who's ever married into the group."

They emerged into the wide entryway and to her right, Holly saw Jared standing next to Simon with Joseph to Simon's right. People milled around between her and the men so they didn't see her approaching. They were deep in conversation, and when Holly got close enough to hear their words, they still had not noticed her.

"She's a rebellious one, Jared. You're going to have to keep a tight rein on her, do you understand me?" asked Simon.

"Yes, Simon, I understand. I'm sure I can control her," said Jared.

"When's her ovo? I'd like to be there for the first one. I can change my schedule," said Simon.

Horrified, Holly didn't come a step closer. She stood there — with people in between her and them — and listened.

"I don't know yet," said Jared.

"Well, you need to find out and let me know. A woman like that can be trouble if you don't put a stop to it immediately. And *I* can put a stop to it."

"Yes, Simon," said Jared.

Simon turned to Joseph. "By the way, Joseph, I'm working on a new revelation. I was going to call it the Messianac Privilege, but then that would exclude you, and I knew you'd want me to include you. It's when I or the Town Chieftain choose to take a woman who's not in ovo. I wish it was already in place, because that woman could certainly use some *severe* guidance, and I do mean severe. No offense, Jared, but I'm not sure if you're up to it."

"I already have some real roughhousers scheduled for her first ovo, Simon, because I was thinking the same thing," said Joseph.

"Good call," said Simon.

Holly noticed that Jared was uncomfortable with the

conversation and was looking for her. She stepped out from behind the tall man, who had inadvertently concealed her, and walked up to him. When he saw her, his eyes lit up and he grabbed both her hands.

"I was afraid you had left or something," he said quietly.

"Oh, I'm not leaving you," she said. "You're my Lord and master."

She had meant it as a joke, but he took it seriously and nodded. "Yes, I am. Are you ready for the reception line?"

"Sure am."

Jared turned his head and looked at Simon. "Simon, we're ready now."

"It's about time," said Simon. Then he cleared his throat, turned on the microphone that was still around his neck, and announced, "The reception line is ready. Please get into a single file line and be orderly like I know you all can be."

Simon's whole demeanor and holier-than-thou attitude, not to mention him acting like he was God Himself, bothered Holly. And while she stood there in the reception line greeting people and having them congratulate her, she could see how Simon worked his magic on the people — especially the women. They fell all over him. Every single woman who walked by hugged him, and most of them kissed him. And it wasn't just a peck on the cheek or the lips, Simon gave each one a long, passionate kiss. And every one reminded Holly of that horrible feeling when he had slipped his tongue between her lips. The slap was humiliating, especially in front of all those people — even though they pretended that they didn't see—but that kiss was the worst part. She felt like she had been violated.

By the time the last person in line congratulated her, Holly's feet were killing her. She leaned over to Jared. "Can we go home now?"

"Home? Holly, no! We have to stay for the reception."

"But it's our wedding. We should be able to leave when we want."

"It's not our wedding, Holly. It's a wedding for the entire town. It's a wedding for all the Children of the Light. And you're one of us now! So let's go get something to eat and mingle!"

Holly gulped, nodded, and followed Jared into the hall where the food was. Two hours later, Holly could barely stand. The simple black flats didn't give her the cushioning or the support of her trusty white tennis shoes, and she could hardly wait to get them off. When she saw that people were starting to leave, she tugged on Jared's hand. "Can we go home *now*?"

Jared shook his head. "No, not yet."

"When, then?"

"Traditionally, the newly wedded couple is always the last to leave."

"Says who?"

"Simon. And you just promised to obey him, so we'll stay until we're the last to go."

Simon Simon Simon. Holly didn't think she could dislike anyone more, but her negative feelings about the man were growing. He was already disrupting their married life, and they hadn't yet been married an entire day. She contrived a smile on her face that she hoped looked authentic and managed not to fall on her face for the next several hours.

When they had said good-bye to the last person, Holly looked up at Jared with relief. *"Now* can we go home?" She felt tired, but she managed to tilt her head, smile at him provocatively, and raise her eyebrows.

"No, of course not." Jared turned around to face the table strewn with leftover food and dirty dishes. "Who would clean up all of this?"

"You surely don't mean *us?"* said Holly, shaking her head.

Jared laughed. "No, silly, of course not!"

Holly sighed with relief. "Oh, good."

Jared took Holly by the shoulders and looked at her. "Not *us*, Holly, *you*. It's *your* job to clean up all of this. Simon says that it's good training for servitude and for obeying your husband *and* him. Every bride does it without complaint."

CHAPTER TWENTY-SEVEN

OLIVIA HAD AN enjoyable morning, finally all to herself and finally able to return to reading her book, which she had put down when she decided to do the book tour. With everything she had to arrange, she hadn't had time to pick it back up again. She enjoyed book signings—being the focus of every-one's attention and all—but she was glad to be home and free of Dean's watchful eye.

Oh, he was a dear for wanting to protect her from danger, and she appreciated that, but there was *no* danger! How silly of him to think so. He had already called three times that morning since leaving for work, and the third time she told him that she was fine and safe and that she wouldn't answer the phone anymore. So she hadn't heard from him since. He had tucked the gun safely away in the table underneath the mirror. It made *him* feel like she was safer, but it meant nothing to her. She didn't need it.

It was the first day she had worn a skirt since they left. She didn't mind wearing pants when the situation called for it, but she felt much more feminine—and like herself—in a skirt or dress.

When she heard the truck in the driveway, and one door slam shut, she smiled and glanced at the clock. It was probably Dean's break time, and since she wouldn't answer the phone, he was coming over to check on her. He was so sweet. Although he was a little overprotective of her, she was so lucky to have him!

She stood up and kept one finger to mark her place in the book. The doorbell rang which surprised her. He was probably just giving her space. Dean was so thoughtful like that. Glancing in the mirror and patting her hair to make sure it looked good for him, she opened the door with a big smile on her face.

Immediately, she knew she had made a mistake. The big burly man with the blue Dallas Cowboys cap, and the tall, thin man with the green John Deere cap, stood right in front of her. The table with the gun inside was too far for her to reach, and she couldn't slam the door in their faces, because the burly man had already put his foot in the way. In the seconds before they grabbed her, she bent the page over where she had been reading and dropped the book.

Before she could scream, the burly man had grabbed her, and the thinner man had stuffed a sock into her mouth. "This is the book with all the lies in it!" The thinner man looked at the book she had dropped and gave it a kick. Olivia turned her head to see where it had gone, and it was under the couch, with only a small piece of it sticking out. Would Dean even see that?

The hedges in her front yard prevented the neighbors from seeing the men force her out to their truck. They pulled her arms behind her back, snapped a pair of handcuffs on, shoved her into the backseat of the truck, and slammed the door. Without a word, they got back into the truck with the burly man driving. He glanced behind him to back up without even looking at her.

Her heart beat wildly, but the whole situation was so unreal that she couldn't really accept what was happening. She closed her eyes and thought about Dean. I'm so sorry, Dean. I didn't take your concerns seriously, and now I'm in trouble. Shaking her head, she realized that he was working a double shift, and since she had asked him not to call, he wouldn't even know she was missing for hours and hours. She could be dead before he even discovered she was gone.

Olivia started coughing and choking with the sock in her mouth. She couldn't get any air into her lungs at all. She bounced around on the seat looking frantic, hoping that the men would notice. The thinner man glanced over his shoulder. "Shut up. Stop pretending you can't breathe!"

The burly man looked in the rearview mirror. "Darryl, I don't think she *can* breathe. Take the sock out of her mouth."

"No, she'll scream, Buck. We can't chance it."

"Darryl, she's choking back there! Can't you see that?" He looked again at Olivia. "Will you promise not to scream if we take the sock out?"

Olivia nodded and leaned forward. Darryl took the sock out of her mouth and held up his hand. "Don't you dare scream or I'll whack you one."

When Olivia finally caught her breath—Darryl watching the whole time—she said, "I won't scream. Please don't put that back in my mouth."

Left alone with her own thoughts for a while, she thought maybe she had an ally in the one called Buck. At least he was reasonable about the sock in her mouth. Maybe she could offer him money or something to set her free.

There was no escaping from the backseat where they had left her. She recognized the doors on the truck as soon as they shoved her in. They called them "suicide doors" because you couldn't open the back door until someone opened the front. No chance of escape there. Her arms behind her made it difficult to get comfortable on the seat— as if you *could* be comfortable when you were being kidnapped. So she worked at trying to get her wrists below her butt and over her legs. Finally, she succeeded. Not that it did her any good though.

An hour later, Buck looked in the rearview mirror and stared at her so long, she was afraid he might drive off the road. "She's a real looker, huh, Darryl?"

Darryl turned his head and nodded. "She is, Buck, she is. Maybe after Carter is through with her, he'll give us a shot."

"We don't have to wait. How would he find out, anyway? *She* wouldn't tell him."

"Don't get any ideas, Buck. You heard Carter. We're not supposed to hurt her or *touch* her. At all."

"But he didn't specifically say we couldn't fuck her, right?"

"Buck, get off it. He said what he said, and he meant not *to touch her at all.*"

Buck glanced in the rearview mirror again. "I dunno, Darryl, if he didn't want us to *fuck* her, I think he would have said that specifically."

"Just stop it, Buck! We're not touching the broad, okay?

We're not touching her! Besides, we don't even know if she's ovo or not!"

"Like that matters," mumbled Buck.

Olivia closed her eyes and cowered into the corner of the backseat. So Buck wasn't an ally after all. She shivered. Oh, Dean, thought Olivia. Please, please call me so you know I'm missing. You've always been my knight in shining armor, and now is your chance to rescue me. *Please* call. She sighed and thought back to the evening they had met.

A friend of hers had fixed them up—it was a cousin of Dean's. She didn't want to go, but the friend had been so convincing about the two of them being perfect for each other. And Ellsworth Bainbridge III—yes, *that* Bainbridge of the Texas Bainbridge oil family—would at the very least be interesting to talk to. Olivia had imagined him dressed in a three-piece suit, arriving in a black limo or maybe a red Jaguar to match her red BMW, and taking her to some ultra-expensive and exclusive place to eat.

And to prepare for the evening that she had in mind, she had worn three-inch spike heels and a blue chiffon evening dress. Of course she had put her makeup on to perfection, as usual. When the doorbell rang and she opened the door, to her surprise she saw a cowboy at the door, complete with cowboy hat and belt and boots, and saw his big truck parked behind her car. She couldn't help herself; she burst out laughing. And to her surprise, he did, too! He saw how she was dressed and how he was dressed, and he cracked up, too! Of course, his good looks hadn't gone unnoticed. Six-four, hard-bodied, short blonde hair and gentle blue eyes.

She felt so delighted at him being the opposite of what

she had expected, she opened her arms at the same time he opened his, and they hugged, a wonderfully close hug. Then, she had kissed him and said, "Now we don't have to wait for the awkwardness of a first kiss, do we?" He opened his truck door for her and gave her another peck on the lips —probably so she wouldn't feel uncomfortable at stealing the first kiss—Dean always was considerate like that.

Olivia found out then that "Ellsworth Bainbridge III" didn't suit him, so he referred to himself as Dean Bainbridge. She and Dean had talked all the way to the restaurant like they had known each other all their lives. He said he had planned on taking her for pizza, but instead, since she was so dressed up, he'd take her to his favorite seafood place. A little dive called The Wharf that had the best steak and lobster this side of Maine. It had become their favorite place to eat.

After that night, they spent every moment together. Within a year, Dean had asked her to marry him. She said that she loved him completely, but she wasn't ready to give up her independence yet. It sounded silly now that she thought about it. Perhaps if she had said yes that time or one of the subsequent times they had talked of marriage, then she wouldn't be in the fix she was in now. Oh, that's a silly thought. But she was allowed silly thoughts at a time like this, wasn't she?

CHAPTER TWENTY-EIGHT

Consummation

DISBELIEVING, HOLLY JUST looked at Jared with her hands on her hips. She thought he was kidding, but he stood there with a bland expression on his face. She shook her head and said, "You're kidding, right?"

"No. And I'd really like to get home, so please start cleaning right away." Then he turned, walked into the other room, and sat down with his back to her.

Closing her eyes to keep the tears from flowing, she slipped off her shoes and got to work. An hour and a half later, she had cleaned and wiped the table, washed, dried, and put away the dishes, and put the leftover food into plastic containers in the refrigerator. She slipped her shoes back on, walked into the room where Jared was reading a Bible, and sank into the chair next to him. "I'm finished, Jared. Let's go home."

Without looking at her, he turned his head to look into

the entryway. "The table looks fine, but there's still flowers all over the floor. You need to clean them up as well."

"No! I'm not going to do it! No! That's too much!"

"I thought it was, too, but Joseph insisted on the flowers, saying that you'd think it was romantic."

Ah, so the red and white roses were Joseph's idea—not Jared being romantic, but Joseph knowing how difficult it would be to clean. Great. Just great. "Well, I'm not doing it, Jared. I'm just not doing it."

Then he looked at her with a serious expression. "You have to. If you don't finish the cleanup, then our marriage will be considered annulled." He shrugged. "You have to."

Holly glared at him, crossed her hands over her chest, and shook her head. "I'm not doing it."

Jared stood up, leaned down to where she was sitting, and just when she thought he was going to kiss her and sweet talk her into doing it, he slapped her across the face. "Yes, you are! Now get up right now, or I'll hit you again."

Holly's mouth was still hanging open from shock when she stood up and looked at him. "I can't believe you did that."

"Simon warned me that I might have to, and Joseph said that if I didn't keep you in line, *he* would. So I did it for your own good."

"For my own good, huh?"

His expression softening, Jared said, "Listen, Holly, I'll tell you what. I'm not supposed to help at all, but I'll do the outside for you. Don't tell anyone."

Holly, feeling shocked into submission, just nodded in agreement. She walked into the other room, retrieved the broom, and started sweeping out the entryway.

Jared walked up to her and grabbed the broom out of her hands. "I need this to sweep up the outside." He opened the front door of the church and before stepping out said, "You're not supposed to use the broom."

When he closed the door behind him, Holly said aloud, "I'm not, am I? We'll see about that." She rushed into the bathroom where she had seen a push broom before. Checking out the window, she saw that Jared was still at the far end of the sidewalk closest to the street.

As fast as she could, she swept the area in front of the window, having to bend down time and again to scrape off the petals that had gotten stuck to the floor with someone's heel. Holly glanced out the window again to see that Jared was only a quarter of the way up the walk. He was holding the broom incorrectly, so it was taking him longer. She finished the entire entryway, and Jared still wasn't finished.

Then she rushed into the inner church sweeping the flowers down the center aisleway. So intent on finishing before he came back in, she almost forgot to check the window again. When she did, he was working on the final six feet from the door of the church. Hurrying, she put the broom back in the bathroom, taking care to pull off the flowers that had gotten caught in the bristles and flushing the evidence down the toilet.

Then she brought a garbage bag from the kitchen,

scooped up the swept flowers in the entryway with her hands, then did the same with the ones in the inside aisle. She was down on her hands and knees picking up the remainder when Jared walked in.

"Get me a bag to put them in, will you?"

"Yeah, sure, Jared. Right away, sir!" She jumped up, ran into the kitchen, and brought him back the bag. He never did catch her sarcasm, but he took the bag and disappeared out the door taking the broom with him. Returning to the floor, she still had ten feet to clear when he walked in and tilted his head to look at her.

"You got this done really fast. How'd you do that?"

"By being *really* motivated to get home," she said. "Now move, so I can finish."

"*Don't* tell me what to do, Holly."

"Yeah, okay, I won't. Sorry."

He stood there a minute more while she looked at the floor and waited. Finally, he walked away after dropping his bag of flowers onto where she was working. Some of them spilled out. She picked them up, then picked up the rest of what she had been working on. When she finished, she tied the tops of each garbage bag and carried them out, one at a time, to the industrial garbage bin in back of the church. She had to stand on her tiptoes, hold the bin open with one hand, and push the unwieldy bag in with the other. Then she stood in front of where he was sitting again and said quietly, "Can we go home now? I'm finished."

Without smiling, he nodded and walked toward the door

of the church. He walked out, without holding the door open for her, and then continued walking to his truck in the parking lot. She thought that he'd at least help her up into the truck, but he didn't and started it before she was even inside. Neither of them spoke on the way home until Holly saw a car with a bright light sweeping the other side of the road.

"What's that car doing?"

"That's the deputy on night duty. He'll patrol the streets all night to make sure everything is secure."

Not another word was said as they drove home. When they arrived there, Jared got out of the truck and walked into the house without even turning on the outside light for her.

What happened to the kind and gentle Jared she had fallen in love with? It was probably Joseph's bad influence and Simon's presence. The irrepressibly optimistic Holly thought that when Simon left, she'd get her old Jared back. She dragged herself into the house, locked the door behind her, walked into his bedroom—where she'd never been before—and flopped onto the bed.

As much as she had wanted to make love to him before their marriage, between the horribly humiliating ceremony, and having to clean the whole church after a long, stressful day, Holly just wanted to go to sleep. And when Jared walked in a few minutes later, that's what she told him.

"Oh, no. We have to consummate the marriage tonight."

"Jared, I just worked incredibly hard for hours, we can

do it in the morning. I'm exhausted."

"Take your clothes off, Holly. We're consummating the marriage tonight. It's not a choice." He walked from the room.

She dutifully took off her clothes and waited for him, naked under the covers. When he stepped into the room again and saw her in the bed, he turned out the light, took off his own clothes, and slid in beside her. Without even a kiss, the act was over in a few minutes. Then he turned over and fell asleep.

In the hours after that, while Holly had plenty of time to think about all the events of the day and night, including "the act" because it certainly couldn't have been called making love, she finally came to the decision that it had been a stressful day for Jared too, and the next time, he would make love to her properly. And still trying to find something to smile about, she fell asleep alone, on her side of the bed, knowing that in the morning, he would go back to being the old Jared that she loved.

When first light of morning woke her, she crept out of bed and into his green and yellow bathroom, where she found his gel toothpaste and put some in her mouth. She didn't want to have morning breath when they made love. He didn't wake for an hour after she returned to bed, but when he stirred, she softly put her hand on his shoulder, leaned into him, and said, "You want another go-round, big boy?"

Jared turned to her, smiled, and took her again, the

same as the previous night, without a kiss or any other hint of affection or foreplay. A few minutes later, he stood up, looked down at her, and said, "Make my breakfast now, will you? And don't say anything to Joseph about sleeping up here in my bedroom. I was supposed to keep you locked downstairs until he approved it."

CHAPTER TWENTY-NINE

THE LAST THREE hours of Dean's first shift was excruciating. He had called Olivia after being at work for an hour; he thought that was reasonable—what if someone had been watching the house and waiting for him to leave? Then he waited two more hours and called again. She complained, but he had still called again after another hour. Olivia had made it clear that she had enough of his watching over her and that she wouldn't accept any more calls from him. Although he was scheduled to work a double, he knew there was no way he could be away from her that long—with everything going on—and that he had to get someone else to cover his second shift.

It took him four phone calls and agreeing to an unusual arrangement to get out of his second eight-hour shift. He and Olivia had to babysit for John and Elizabeth Riley's three children on the following Saturday night. Olivia wouldn't mind. They had discussed having children—that is, if she would ever agree to marry him. She always seemed to have a reason to delay it. It didn't bother him, though, because he knew that her heart beat only for him, as his did for her, but still, he wished that she would agree sometime soon.

Flipping open his cell phone after stepping into his truck, he was going to call her, but decided not to. It was only a fifteen-minute drive to her place. He could wait that long so as not to aggravate her with another call.

During the drive to her house, he felt uncomfortable, but thought it was his nerves—or his overactive imagination as Olivia put it. Then when he pulled into the driveway behind her red BMW, the feeling of wrong-ness washed over him. Everything looked fine, but he knew in his heart that it wasn't.

Dean jumped out of his truck, ran to the front door, and found it unlocked. Although Olivia discounted all his fears, she would never have left the door unlocked. After pulling his gun out of its holster, he crept inside. Nothing looked out of order—except that her book stuck out from beneath the couch. Before bending down to pick it up, he walked to the table beneath the mirror and slowly opened the drawer. The gun was still there. Untouched. He didn't want to call out her name in case they were still somehow in the house, so he methodically inspected every room and every closet. No Olivia and no one else either.

He re-holstered his gun and leaned down to pick up her book. When he flipped through the pages, he found that one of them was bent over—something Olivia would *never* do to any book. It was the only clue she could leave him—as if he needed to know who had taken her. Dean tried calling her, just in case, but her phone was on the coffee table in front of the couch, singing away. As he walked out the door, he called his friend Carlos.

"Carlos? . . . They've got her, man. . . . Yes, I'm sure. . . . No, I have no proof. . . . I know that the Rangers can't help me without proof, but— . . . No, Carlos, I can't let you do that. . . . It's not your battle. . . . Yes, of course I would, but — . . . Well, if you know of any others— . . . Okay, anything you can do would be great. I appreciate it, man. . . . I'll call you when I get close to Amarillo. . . . Bye."

Dean had considered trying to rescue Olivia using her red BMW and having a couple of savvy women go into the cult and create a diversion so Dean could get in there unnoticed. But he had rejected that idea as too risky. Any plan would be risky, but putting more women at risk in a place like that was more than Dean could handle. So he hopped into his truck, checked the gas, and sped off. Although he would have liked to go over the videos that they had shot of Plenty to give him a better idea of what he was heading into, he would have to go by memory from when they visited—and the information that Carlos might have.

Dean tried to go over the timing in his head. He had called her at eight o'clock, ten o'clock, and eleven o'clock. So eleven o'clock was the earliest they could have come for her. That meant they might have a four and a half hour lead on him—which meant there was no way he could catch them before they got back to the cult headquarters. He could try to fly, but it would have to be standby, and if he couldn't get on a flight, then he would be that much further behind. No, driving was the only way. He just had to hope that once he got to Amarillo and got everything in place, it wouldn't be too late.

There was always the chance that they had already killed

her and stashed her body someplace, but Dean didn't think so. With Carter Weeks or de la Luz—whatever he wanted to call himself—his ego was too big to let her get away with writing that book without him admonishing her for it in person. It was the admonishment part that scared Dean. The so-called Messiah wasn't rational, and there was no telling what he might do to Olivia. Dean knew that he had to get there as quickly as possible.

CHAPTER THIRTY

Cooking, Watching, Listening

FEELING USED AND discouraged, Holly started the coffee and then walked downstairs to get dressed. When she returned upstairs, Jared was on his cell phone. She had never seen him use it before and had never seen it on him, so it made her wonder where he kept it. That thought led to the next, and she wondered where *her* cell phone had gone.

Taking the pancake mix out of the pantry, she measured out the ingredients, put them in a bowl, and started beating it to get the lumps out. Then she took the frying pan and put it on the burner to warm up. From the refrigerator, she took a pat of butter and put it on the pan. While she waited for the pan to heat, she poured two cups of coffee and gave one to Jared. After checking to see if the pan was hot enough—it wasn't—she put silverware on the table and sat down with Jared.

He hung up his phone, looked up at her crossly, and

said, "Where's my breakfast?"

Holly laughed. "You're joking, right?"

"No. I told you to cook my breakfast and all I see is that you're sitting at the table drinking coffee when you should be waiting on me."

"Well, excuuuse me! I'm *waiting* for the pan to get hot. Can't you smell the butter?"

"Just hurry up."

Holly took one more sip of coffee, stood up, put the coffee on the counter where she could reach it, and checked the pan. As she poured the pancake batter into the frying pan, she glanced over at Jared who was gazing out the window looking perfectly innocent. What was going on, she wondered. What had happened to make Jared act this way? She had never thought to check for a pancake turner in the drawers, but luckily, when she pawed through a drawer full of miscellaneous kitchen implements, she found one. While flipping the pancakes over, she shook her head at the change in Jared. When they were finished, she put all of them on a plate for Jared, brought them to him, and then brought him the syrup. He started eating without even as much as a thank you or a glance in her direction.

Holly closed her eyes, sighed, and poured more pancake batter into the pan. She glanced over at him and asked, "Is that enough or do you want more?"

"That's enough."

Still no thank you, she mused. She flipped the pancakes, waited for them to cook, turned off the burner, put the remaining pancakes on a plate, and sat at the table. The pancakes were good, and she was hungry. A minute later, the front door opened, and Joseph walked into the room.

"Jared," he said. He looked Holly up and down but didn't address her. Then he sat at the table.

"You want some pancakes?" asked Jared.

"Yeah, they smell good. At least she can cook."

"Holly, make Joseph some pancakes."

After taking one more bite of pancake, she stood up, turned the burner back on, and made up some more batter. Then she poured the batter into the frying pan and sat down to eat another bite and wait to flip them over.

"I told you to make Joseph some pancakes!" said Jared, raising his voice.

If Joseph hadn't been there, she would have said, "Hel-looo! They're on the stove!" But with him there, she merely said, "They're on the stove." After another bite, she stood up, flipped them over, and thought better of sitting back down again, so she sipped her coffee and waited for the pancakes to finish. When they did, she put them on a plate and put them in front of Joseph. "Would you like some coffee, Joseph?"

"Yes, but you should have asked me when I first came in!" He dug into the pancakes.

She poured him some coffee and resisted the urge to spill it in his lap. While in college, she had been a waitress at a small diner near campus. Since college boys would be boys, the management knew that if a waitress was driven to deliberately spill something, the customer definitely deserved it. The manager would apologize and fawn all over the customer and whoever he was with, and after they left he would ask the waitress what they had done. Usually the manager said, "Good call" and walked away. But doing that to Joseph would not be a good call. So she kept quiet and sat down to finish her pancakes which were not even half eaten.

"Holly, can you strip the bed in my room and put the sheets in the washer downstairs?"

"Sure, Jared." And she put another bite into her mouth.

"I mean *now*!"

"Can't I finish eating, please?" She stuffed a big bite of pancake in her mouth in case he said no, which he did. So she gulped down the last of the coffee, walked into the bedroom, and started ripping the sheets off the bed. She was furious. The bedroom was only a few feet from the kitchen, so Holly could hear every word of the conversation between Joseph and Jared. They talked like she wasn't even there.

"So are you taking Simon's advice about how to treat her?"

"You were here. You saw me," said Jared defensively.

"I didn't know if that was for my benefit or not."

"No, of course not," said Jared. "I don't want to lose her."

Holly had finished with the sheets and now walked out of the room and opened the door to the basement. The conversation stopped, but they should have known she could hear everything from the bedroom. That was a curious comment, thought Holly as she walked down the stairs. Then, the basement door closed behind her, but she didn't hear the deadbolt. Ah, so they didn't want her to hear the rest of the conversation. Okay, then! Thank you, Marina!

She placed the sheets on the table, walked over to the heater doors, opened them, and slowly pulled the cord so she could hear through the vent. They weren't whispering, so again, she could hear every word.

"So you gave her the ovo test this morning?" asked Joseph.

"No, not yet."

"It could be today, man! You're making me miss out! You make sure she takes the test today and let me know! I did you this big favor of arresting her—I at least need to get something for it."

"All right, Joseph," said Jared. "Listen, I need to talk to you about something."

"What now, little brother?"

"I want to leave her alone in the house without locking her in the basement."

"No way! She'll take off on you!"

"Joseph, we took all the gas out of her car. How's she going to take off?"

Holly rocked back on her heels. So Susan had been telling the truth after all. That gave her a sick feeling inside. And the something that Joseph was going to get was having sex with me, thought Holly. So no First Rites. Susan was right about that as well. She shook her head. I'm sorry I doubted you, Susan.

"Okay, I'll let you, but we have to try an experiment first to see if she still wants to leave."

"I told you that she said she loved me."

"She could have just been saying that. She could be faking the whole thing. Did she resist when you consummated the marriage last night?"

"Not at all, and she wanted to again this morning. What kind of experiment? I won't do anything where she can get hurt."

"We'll put the gas back in the car, leave her alone, and put the keys out where she can see them—but not someplace so obvious that she knows it's a setup. Then we'll wait and see if she tries to run—I'll have a couple boys waiting close by, just in case."

"Fine, I'll try it. But how can I stop her from seeing me put the gas back in the car? I don't want her to know that I did anything like that. It would be like I didn't trust her."

"That's *your* problem, little brother. I'm sure you'll come up with something. When do you want to do it? You know tomorrow you have three appointments in a row."

"Today then, it has to be today."

"All right, let me know when you have everything set up and you leave the house."

When Holly heard someone's chair scooting across the floor, she pulled the vent cord, closed the sliding doors, and hurried to put the sheets into the washer on the other side of the room. She had just started the machine when the basement door opened above.

"Holly!" called Jared.

"Yes, Jared, I'm still down here."

"Listen, Holly, sometimes the spin cycle makes the machine jump out of place. I don't want water to get all over. Will you stay down there until the clothes go into the dryer?"

"Oh, can't I come up and finish my breakfast first?" Holly figured that if she gave in too easily, he might suspect something.

"You can finish later! Just stay down there!" She heard him shut the door hard—just this side of a slam—and heard the bolt slide into place.

CHAPTER THIRTY-ONE

THEY HAD BEEN driving for two hours, with Olivia huddled in the backseat, and Buck occasionally turning his head to give her a leering look. The last time he had looked, he had nodded his head and then turned to Darryl. "I need to get some gas. You hungry?"

"Yeah, I'm starved."

Buck glanced back at her again and raised his eyebrows. "Great. I'll get off at the next exit." The next exit was in a few miles, and Buck pulled off the highway and into a gas station. He reached into his pocket and handed some money to Darryl. "You get the food, and I'll get gas. Get some for the bitch, too. And get me some chocolate candy. And a beer."

"You can't drink and drive, Buck. All we need is to get pulled over if some cop sees you with the can."

"Then buy me a large coke, too, and I'll pour it in there. No one will notice. Go on, Darryl."

Darryl walked away shaking his head, and when Buck saw the station door close and Darryl disappear, he jumped out of the truck, opened the back door, climbed into the backseat, and closed the door behind him. The front door remained open.

"Come on, bitch. I'm going to take care of business." He grabbed her legs and pulled them out from under her, hitting her head on the arm rest. She started hitting him with her handcuffed hands and was about to scream, until he pushed her hands over her head. "You scream, and I'll hurt you bad. I mean it. Shut up and cooperate. How'd you get your hands undone, anyway?"

Olivia wouldn't scream, but she didn't intend to cooperate, either. She tried turning from side to side beneath him, but he put more weight on her and held her down. With one hand, he held her handcuffed hands over her head so she couldn't hit him anymore, and with the other hand and his knees, he spread her legs. Her skirt was already up around her waist, and he was fumbling trying to get his penis out of his pants, when the side door opened and Darryl looked in.

"Buck! Dammit! Get off her!"

"Shut up, Darryl, it'll only take a minute."

Olivia couldn't move; Buck had her arms pinned, and his whole weight was on her. His penis was out of his pants and he was almost there. But Darryl ran around the truck, opened the door, and pulled Buck off. Olivia pulled her skirt down, tucked her feet beneath her, and resumed huddling against the door of the truck while the two men scuffled outside. She didn't think skinny Darryl could take on Buck, but he somehow bested him. Perhaps it was that Buck was at a disadvantage with his erect penis sticking straight out of his pants.

Buck slammed the back door and climbed into the front

seat in a huff. When Darryl climbed in, Buck glared at him. "What'd you come back for, anyway? And where's the food?"

"You didn't tell me what you wanted."

"Anything! It could have been anything! I can't believe you came back here for that." He hit the steering wheel, shook his head violently, and snorted. "Well, go on now and get it!"

Olivia froze in the backseat. If Darryl left again, she knew that she couldn't stop Buck the next time. If there was only some way she could prevent the "next time." But she knew there wasn't. She was a helpless victim. It struck her funny, though. Not for one moment in her whole entire life had Olivia ever considered herself a helpless victim. She was a woman who made things happen in her life, not a woman whom things happened to. So why was this happening to her now, she wondered.

Darryl laughed. "There's no way I'm leaving you alone with her again, Buck. I'm not an idiot! You want food? You go get it yourself!"

"I thought you were starved. Where's *your* food?"

"I was polite and came back to ask you what you wanted before I got my own. So here's your money back and more of mine. Get me a ham sandwich."

Buck grabbed the money out of Darryl's hand and stomped off before turning back and shouting, "You can starve as far as I'm concerned, Darryl! And put some gas in the truck, will ya?"

Before Darryl exited the truck, Olivia said, "Thank you."

Darryl ignored her and began pumping gas. A few minutes later, Buck came back with a paper bag and a large plastic cup of coke in his hands. He stopped at the garbage can, dumped the coke out, and then got into the truck. After closing the door, he poured the beer from the can into the empty cup. Then he took out a sandwich and started eating the first half. When Darryl stuck his head in the window, Buck said, "It's already paid for. Get in. Let's get out of here." Then he reached in the bag, pulled out another sandwich and threw it in the backseat. "That's for you. You need to get your strength up, 'cause I'm going to have you yet. And don't you dare give any food to *him*, or I'll hurt you. I swear I'll hurt you bad."

Darryl had climbed into the truck and heard what Buck said. "You really didn't get me anything, Buck? You pig!"

"You hungry? Go buy it yourself!" He gave Darryl a big grin that showed food stuck in his front teeth.

As Buck put the truck in gear and drove out of the gas station, Darryl looked around like he was trying to find someone to buy it for him. "There! There's a Burger Giant drive-thru. Pull in there!"

Buck laughed. "That would defeat the whole purpose, wouldn't it?"

By then, Olivia had finished half the sandwich. Buck had threatened her, but she already knew where his head was at; and Darryl had saved her. She wrapped up the other half of the sandwich and passed it over the right-hand side of the seat to Darryl. Buck glared at her.

CHAPTER THIRTY-TWO

Figuring It All Out

HOLLY DIDN'T KNOW how long it would take for him to put the gas back in her tank, but if he had drained it all out, and it sounded like he had, then it would take at least ten minutes. She lay down on the bed to wait and think about what had happened since the wedding and about the conversation she had just heard.

Remembering Simon sliding his tongue between her lips grossed her out and made her realize what a fool she had been to think she could possibly have a normal marriage to Jared. And Joseph asking about ovo—obviously Jared was *not* going to claim First Rites. And not to mention Joseph saying that Jared had three appointments tomorrow. "Appointments" were their euphemism for "procreating." And procreating was their euphemism for having sex with anything that bleeds, she thought bitterly. How could she have been so wrong about Jared?

Her strong feelings of longing and love for Jared drained out of her as fast as they had first appeared. Why had they appeared, she wondered. Then she remembered something that she had studied in a psychology class — something called Stockholm Syndrome, where a hostage or a victim, starts to identify with their captor. In her own case, Holly thought, it was the juxtaposition of Joseph and Jared. Joseph being mean to her and Jared being kind. Of course, now she knew that all that had been a setup, but still it had affected her more than she realized. And the moment when she had "fallen" for Jared — if you could call it that, now that she had come to her senses — was when Joseph was about to rape her and Jared saved her and chased him off.

It was classic good cop–bad cop stuff from television programs, and she had fallen for it. Granted, Joseph really was a jerk, and up until yesterday, Jared really was kind; but still, she had fallen for it and here she was *married* to her erstwhile captor. Maybe not so erstwhile — she was still locked in the basement.

Now that her perspective had come round again to wanting — no, needing — to escape, she had to make plans. Immediately. The first, naturally, was to pass the test they were setting up for her with the car. From there, she had to bide her time to make sure that she could get away clean. If she attempted to escape and failed, life could get a whole lot worse for her. Joseph — and not to mention Simon — would make sure of that.

Her plan had to be perfect, and it might take her a while to come up with one. She didn't have forever to think about it though. There was a time limit: ovo, as they called it. When was her next one? Putting her hand on her stomach, she thought, more to the point, when was this one? Four days before, she had felt a slight cramp on her left side, which she had always thought meant she was ovulating, but it had never mattered before. Now she wondered how long it lasted. She had no idea how those ovo tests worked but guessed there was a chance she would register positive if she took it now. She shuddered thinking of a ten-man gang bang. The first man of course would be Joseph. If Jared wanted her to take the test today, she would try to delay until at least tonight.

The whole ovo thing brought to mind something that should have come to mind long ago. First Rites. Even if Jared had claimed them, what good would it have done her? It would only have given her one extra month before the onslaught began. She had an IUD—an intra-uterine-device—which prevented pregnancy. There was no way she would get pregnant, and no way she would ever tell them why. Perhaps there were children in her future, but not now and not fathered by this group of crazies.

Now that she had her mind—and her heart—back, she had to be careful not to give herself away. She still had to pretend she was at least halfway going along with all the craziness, so they wouldn't expect her to run. She had to be convincing, and she couldn't tell anyone.

At one time she thought she might have been able to trust Marina, but Marina was so young and so brainwashed to believe that the only way to get to heaven was to do what these men expected of her. Susan, there was no way she could ever trust her—even after the horrible story that she told about Joseph. Susan was "one of them." No, Holly was in this alone and could trust no one except herself.

What happened to her clothes, she wondered. If she actually had to run, these long skirts that she was wearing certainly wouldn't be conducive to that. Sitting up on the bed, she looked around the room but didn't see them. Then she opened the drawer of the nightstand next to the bed, and she smiled. Her clothes weren't there, but the handcuffs that had been on her wrists were. And they were open, ready to slip on an unsuspecting person—an unsuspecting person who wasn't her.

The bolt slid out of place, the basement door opened, and Jared called down, "Holly! Come finish your breakfast!"

She put the sheets in the dryer and walked up the stairs, trying to keep the grin off her face. After being locked in the basement again, she shouldn't be happy. So she acted it.

"Why'd you lock me in, Jared? I'm your wife! Did you really think that I'd leave just like that? Don't you trust me?" Holly had her hands on her hips and her eyes narrowed at him.

"Yes, yes, of course I trust you. I'm sorry. Just habit, I guess. I won't do it again."

She allowed herself to soften her gaze. "Jared, I thought you loved me. Don't you *love* me?"

He put his hands on her shoulders. "Yes. Yes, of course I love you."

"Then why have you been treating me so badly? I feel like you don't even like me anymore."

Jared looked down. "I'm treating you like this because I *do* love you. I don't want to lose you."

Holly was about to say that she had already heard him say that when she realized that would give her secret surveillance away. So instead, she said, "I don't understand."

"Joseph had already told Simon what a rebel you were and not really one of us. And I already told you that Simon had warned me that I *must* keep you in line, or *he* would take care of you himself."

"That's right. You did tell me that the night of our wedding. Oh, dear."

"I know!" He put his hands on her shoulders again. "I don't want to lose you, Holly. I'll do anything I have to do to keep you — even treat you badly if I have to."

Holly set her mouth to try to keep from laughing at how stupid it all sounded. She took a deep breath. "All right, I understand. Too bad I can't help you by being more cooperative, but some of the stuff that goes on here is downright crazy." She shrugged.

"Don't ever say that in front of anyone but me! Don't ever say that again at all! That's exactly what would get you into the kind of trouble that Simon—or Joseph—would want to fix. Which reminds me, you need to take an ovo test. Why don't you take it now?"

Holly wanted to make him sweat. "Why do I need to take an ovo test? I thought you were going to claim First Rites."

"That was only a threat to Joseph. The only way I could get him to arrest you"—he nodded his head at her—"you know, so I could marry you, was to promise him that I wouldn't claim First Rites. It was a threat, but Joseph knew that I wouldn't go back on my word." Holly just looked at him, expressionless, so he continued. "And you have to take the ovo test, so Joseph knows when to set up the appointments for procreating."

Holly couldn't help herself. "Ten men. In one day. That's the kind of stuff that is just crazy."

She could see that her comment had set Jared off. "Holly, *that's* how women get to the Promised Land! You want to get there, don't you? It's not crazy! Simon had a revelation! And you promised in our wedding ceremony to obey the tenets of the church."

Immediately, she knew she had gone too far, so she put her head down so she didn't have to look him in the eye and lie to him. "Yes, Jared, of course I want to go to the Promised Land."

Jared let out a breath of relief. "Oh, good. You had me worried there for a minute. Anyway, take the ovo test and leave it in the bathroom so I can see it. Simon wants to know your schedule so he can be here for your next one."

It took all of Holly's might not to let her head jerk up and scream that there was no way she was going to let Simon touch her, but instead, she slowly nodded her head. "All right."

"You know, Holly, it's a big compliment for Simon to want to attend your ovo. He doesn't *honor* everyone like that. He even said he'd make a special trip out here. You should feel privileged."

You bet I do, thought Holly. But she stayed silent, nodded her head, and kept looking down.

"All right, I'm glad we understand each other now." He stepped forward, put his arms around her, and gave her a quick hug. She forced herself to hug him back. "Now go take the ovo test for me, so I can tell Joseph it's done."

"I'll do it later."

He pulled away from her and held her tightly by the shoulders. "Holly! This is what I mean! You have to listen to me and do what I tell you to do. That's what obeying me means! Now go do it *now*!"

"I can't!" she screamed and pulled away from him.

"Why not?"

"Because I just went to the bathroom, and I couldn't possibly squeeze out another drop of pee. It's going to have to wait."

Jared chuckled. "Oh. Okay. I can understand that. Great, later is fine. I've got to go to work now. See you later." He leaned forward and gave her a kiss on the cheek, then opened the door and stepped out. Holly didn't have time to move an inch before the door opened again. "Be sure to wash and dry all the dishes. Bye!"

CHAPTER THIRTY-THREE

BUCK WATCHED DARRYL scarf down the sandwich. He was hungry. Good. Let him stay that way. Buck noisily finished his sandwich, saying "Mmmmm mmmmm good," as he crushed the paper wrapping in his hand in front of Darryl's face. Darryl pushed the hand away. Then Buck reached into the paper bag beside him and took out another sandwich. "Too bad you didn't know about this one!" Darryl tried to grab it out of Buck's hand, but Buck switched it to his left hand where Darryl couldn't reach.

The truck entered freeway traffic, and Buck continued eating the sandwich slowly and noisily. Every once in a while, he would look at Darryl, and if Darryl looked his way, he would open his mouth and show him the half chewed up food. After a couple of times, though, whenever he turned his head, Darryl would look out the window.

When Buck finished the sandwich, he felt disappointed that he couldn't torture Darryl any longer. His disappointment turned rapidly to anger at not being able to fuck the woman. He glanced in the backseat at her cowering in the corner behind Darryl and thought about how sweet it would have been. Why did Darryl have to be so intent on listening to Carter? No one had to know! Darryl could have fucked her too. He gripped the steering wheel tighter, pursed his lips, and exhaled hard through his nose. When the anger had built up so much that he couldn't take it anymore, he balled up his fist and hit the dashboard as hard as he could.

"Dammit, Darryl, why wouldn't you let me fuck her?"

Darryl didn't even look at him and replied in a monotone voice. "Because in Carter's revelation, it said that we should bring her back to him without touching her."

"Carter's *revelation*. Honestly, Darryl, how can you believe that crap? Carter wants something and suddenly he has a revelation to give him that thing. Messianic Privilege? Everyone else has to wait for ovo to be with women, but Carter has *Messianic Privilege*! You honestly believe that he had a revelation that told him that it was okay for *him* to do that and no one else?"

Buck didn't wait for an answer, he just continued. "Give me a fucking break! And what about his revelation regarding young girls? It started with only married women or women over eighteen years old who had the ten men a day during ovo. Then Carter saw a young girl that he wanted, so suddenly he has a revelation that as soon as a girl gets on the rag men can have her during ovo."

"Not ten men, though." Darryl looked at him.

"Five men for a girl that young? Come on, Darryl. You really think that's right? Those girls should still be playing with dolls, not men."

"I don't see *you* turning down any fourteen-year-olds." Darryl crossed his arms.

"I may not turn them down, but how do you know if I'm actually *doing* them?"

"I don't believe that, Buck."

"Believe what you want, Darryl, but unlike Carter, I prefer my women *full grown*." He glanced back at Olivia and then continued. "And you know as well as I do that whenever we turn a woman down, Carter puts a black mark on our name."

"So what's your point?"

"My point is that Carter is making this stuff up as he goes! Revelations! It's all bull shit."

"Just shut up, Buck. I don't want to hear any more of your heresy. Carter is the Messiah, and if you don't believe that, then it's your problem, not mine. I don't want to hear any more about it. And if you hate it so much, then you should leave!"

"I intend to!" Still seething, Buck hit the dashboard again.

An hour later, he was cooling off—and changing his mind. He *liked* getting laid every day or almost every day. Sometimes even more than once in a day. One time, he had three women in one day! And he had performed quite admirably with all three, even if he did have to say so himself. Woo hoo! What a great day that was! Sometimes, Carter would give him a note with his assignments that said he should rough the women up. Buck always especially enjoyed those. It gave a little extra excitement to the act. He didn't know why Carter did that, but he imagined that the women had disappointed him in some way or done something that Carter frowned upon. And Carter frowned upon a lot.

They were all required to attend church services every Sunday. Often, Carter would announce something to do on one Sunday and change his mind a week or two later to do something completely different, or even the exact opposite. Buck thought he should bring that up to Darryl, but when he glanced over at him, Darryl still sat with his arms crossed. Naw, Darryl really thought that jerk Carter was the Messiah. Buck realized that no matter what he said to him or how he tried to change his mind, Darryl wouldn't budge. He was brainwashed. That idiot Darryl would do anything that Carter asked him to. He'd probably even suck Carter's dick if Carter asked him. That made Buck laugh, making Darryl and even the woman in the back look at him.

Buck took another good, long look at her. She was beautiful—especially beautiful cowering in the back like that. As long as he had decided to stay in Plenty for a while, he might somehow arrange to fuck her after all. Perhaps Carter would have a new revelation that he and Darryl should be rewarded for their efforts of bringing the woman back in one piece. A piece for a piece! That made Buck laugh again. Darryl glared at him, but Buck didn't care.

CHAPTER THIRTY-FOUR

Mission Accomplished

SITTING DOWN AT the table, Holly put a mouthful of cold pancake into her mouth and spit it out. Yuck. She threw the rest out and, since she was still hungry, made up more batter and poured herself another cup of coffee while she waited for the pan to get hot again. It was then that she realized she wasn't locked in the basement and was alone in the house. Although she knew about the test they had set up for her, the "freedom" still gave her a funny feeling. Looking around the room, she wondered where Jared would have put the keys so they weren't obvious. They weren't out anywhere that she could see — at least, not in the kitchen. Would he have put them in another room — maybe the bedroom?

After finishing her pancakes, she sipped her coffee and wondered again about where the keys could be. She kept wondering as she washed the dishes. After she finished, she opened the drawer where the towels were, pulled one out, and spotted the keys nestled underneath. Very clever, Jared. Tell me to wash and dry the dishes, and leave the keys with the towels. It might not have been so obvious if she hadn't known it was all planned in advance.

Now what? Do what she had planned, or use the time to explore the house, knowing that no one would interrupt her? If they were going to give her enough rope to hang herself with, as they say, first she would walk away from the rope to see what else she could come up with that might aid in her ultimate escape.

Looking around the kitchen, she started with the pantry, which was completely empty except for the groceries that Susan had brought. She stepped out of the pantry and then turned to the drawers beneath the counter. Holly opened a drawer that she had opened before, then closed it without searching it. If she opened drawers or cabinets in the kitchen, it wouldn't arouse any suspicion, so she could do that anytime. It would be better for now to start in another part of the house.

The formal dining room had a sideboard and a hutch made of glass and wood. Most of the drawers and compartments were empty, and the ones that weren't didn't contain anything of any use. Holly didn't know exactly what she was looking for, but she'd know it when she saw it. As she started to walk into Jared's bedroom, she turned to gaze at the other side of the living room. She'd never ventured into any of those rooms—not that she had the opportunity up until now—so she walked over there. Peeking into each room, she found four more bedrooms. Why would one man need such a huge house with five upstairs bedrooms and a bedroom downstairs?

Starting at the farthest one, she began to search the dressers. Every single drawer in every single dresser was empty—same with the desks. The rooms were also exactly alike. Bunk beds with colorful print bedspreads, two desks, and two dressers. Wallpaper covered the walls with cartoon characters running, jumping, and playing. They were happy rooms, perfect for children. Walking toward Jared's bedroom to give it a quick search, she wondered what the house would be like full of children. And that happy thought gave way to a more gloomy one—children who would believe in the same ideals that their parents did: gang-banging every woman who was ovo.

Jared's drawers were all full, and it took some time to go through each one thoroughly. There were some boxes up high in his closet, and she had to get a chair to reach them. But there was absolutely nothing she could use to aid in her escape.

Dejected, she walked back into the kitchen, picked up her car keys, and with her head held high, walked out the door. After unlocking her car door, she sat inside for the first time in a week. When she turned the key, the engine started up right away. She knew it would, though, because she had just bought a new battery the week before. Without wasting a second, after she checked that the parking brake was on, she jumped out of the car before Joseph's men would have time to catch her in it.

Holly closed the door, and with arms swinging at her sides, she headed toward Jared's gas station across the street. There were no cars getting gas, which she was grateful for, and when she opened the door and walked inside, Jared had a funny expression on his face. She knew that he had been watching the car all morning, and now seeing her there in front of him, he didn't know what to think.

"What are you doing here, Holly?"

"My car hasn't been started in a week, and I wanted to make sure that the battery didn't die. I left it running over there, but I wanted to let you know so you didn't think that I was taking off or anything." She shrugged. "That's all."

"You don't need to do that. I'll take care of the car from now on. It's my job to handle the automobiles. Okay?"

"Sure, Jared, no problem."

"You can go back home now. Be sure to turn off the engine, though."

"Sure. See ya later." Holly opened the door and started walking out when Jared called her back.

"I forgot to tell you. Don't cook dinner tonight. We'll eat at Joseph's and get our wedding gifts. I'll call him now to confirm." Jared pulled his cell phone out from under the counter and placed the call.

Holly, who had been half out the door, turned, came back inside, and started looking at the snacks that were on the end rack, closest to the counter. She knew that the first words that Jared would speak to Joseph would not be about dinner.

"Hey, Joseph. . . . Yeah, car's still there. . . . No, everything's fine. I just wanted to tell you that we would be over for dinner tonight. . . . So you can call your troops off. . . . Yeah. . . . See ya later. Bye."

"Can I have these, Jared?" Holly held up a package of corn chips.

Jared nodded. "Yeah."

She glanced around and then looked at Jared. "Hey, do you have any magazines in here?"

"No, absolutely not! We don't carry the trashy magazines and newspapers from the outside world!"

"Okay, see ya, Jared." She made a concerted effort not to shake her head or say anything disparaging. Let it go, let it go, let it go, she told herself.

"I'll be home just after five."

"See ya then."

Satisfied with passing her test, she walked out the door in time to see two cars pull away—one in each direction. She was certain they were Joseph's goons. Another problem solved, she thought. After crossing the street, she climbed back into the car but didn't turn it off right away. She opened the center compartment and there was her cell phone. It was dead, though, and her charger was in the trunk with her suitcase. Then she opened the glove compartment, shuffled through the maps, papers, and napkins in there, and pulled out a key from the bottom. Her extra key to the car! Exactly what she needed. Her registration and license weren't in there, but oh well. They could be replaced as soon as she was free.

She slipped the key into her pocket, turned off the engine, and walked inside the house with a triumphant smile on her face. As she came through the door into the kitchen, suddenly, from nowhere, she realized what it was she had been searching for—what she would need for her escape. A gun.

CHAPTER THIRTY-FIVE

THE TRUCK SPED down the highway at ninety miles an hour. Dean decided that he would risk getting pulled over to get there sooner. And *if* he did get pulled over, there was always the chance the cop would let him go when Dean showed him his badge. Not every cop gave every other cop professional courtesy, but some did. For Dean, it depended on the circumstances. If a guy was driving drunk, Dean didn't care who it was, Dean would write him up and send him to jail. One time, however, it was the mayor; and Dean arranged to have someone drive the guy and his car home. But he warned him that he wouldn't let him off if it happened again. It would have been a sticky situation if he had ever caught the guy again, but luckily, he hadn't.

Dean had been trapped in that kind of crossfire before. He remembered well why he had gotten "excused" from service with the Texas Rangers—the reason he had ultimately decided to move to Arizona. In filling in for someone else, he had been asked to provide special security for an elected official. That part was fine; Dean had done it before, and besides, it was part of the job. Dean didn't mind.

But when that elected official did something extremely illegal during the evening—expecting Dean to look away or ignore it—that was more than Dean could take. The use of illegal drugs wasn't exactly under his jurisdiction, but still, it was a crime that he couldn't ignore. If it had been the guy smoking a little pot, he would have easily overlooked it. Some of the guys he worked with smoked pot, and it was no big deal. But this guy was using cocaine, and that wasn't right. He reported the man to his superior officer, who, instead of siding with Dean, had immediately suspended him, and later released him, "due to staffing overages."

Everyone knew that Dean had gotten a raw deal, but they couldn't do anything about it. After that, his friend Carlos and a couple of others that Dean was close to, always made excuses when it was their turn to provide security for that same official. Dean never found out whether his superior officer was on the take from the elected official or not, but shortly after Dean was let go, his former superior officer left the Rangers and accepted a position in the official's office.

Initially, Dean felt angry and bitter about it. But after meeting Olivia in Arizona, he realized that it was the best thing that could have happened to him. If he hadn't been on duty that night with the official, and if he hadn't seen what he had seen, and if he hadn't reported it and subsequently gotten "excused," then he would never have met Olivia. And Olivia was his whole life now.

Dean remembered well the night they had met. It was the best first date he had ever had. It was the *last* first date that he'd *ever* have. There was an instant attraction between them—connection, some people called it. But it was so strong that it was palpable, electrifying even. Magical. After that they spent all their free time together. He had known immediately that she was the woman for him. When he had asked her to marry him before the year was out, he wasn't surprised when she said no. Disappointed? Yes. Surprised? No.

Olivia was the most independent woman anyone could ever meet. It was one of the things he loved most about her. She didn't need a man to take care of her, support her, coddle her, protect her, or tell her that she was always right. Olivia usually *was* right! She was not the kind of woman who asked if her butt looked fat. It wasn't, and she knew it and didn't need to ask. As far as Dean was concerned, Olivia's beauty surpassed any other woman he had ever seen— including movie stars and Miss America. She was a tall, statuesque blonde, with large, deep-set blue eyes, and all the grace of a swan. And it wasn't just her looks—Olivia was tough and confident, and she could accomplish anything she set her mind to. That thought made Dean frown. If she hadn't been so *overconfident*, she wouldn't be in the fix she was in now. He couldn't help thinking that maybe if he had pushed for them to be married, she wouldn't be kidnapped and in danger. But that wasn't realistic. Even if she was already his wife, it wouldn't have made any difference to Carter Weeks de la Luz.

CHAPTER THIRTY-SIX

Searching

HOLLY HAD HOPED for hot chocolate, but couldn't find any. So, sitting at the kitchen table with yet another cup of coffee, she just wanted to relax and think. There was a hook on the wall by the door where she had put her keys. They looked like they belonged there. Jared had no reason to take them away since she passed the test. Still, she was grateful for an extra key—just in case.

She had several hours before Jared returned home, and she must take advantage of them. There were some places that she had forgotten to look—like under things, on top of things, and between the mattresses. Also, she still had to finish searching the kitchen and bathrooms. After washing her cup and cleaning the coffee machine, she headed for the main upstairs bathroom—the nearest one off the living room.

Under the sink were only cleaning supplies, and the

drawers were all empty. The large linen closet had several sets of towels and another set of sheets, but no gun or anything else useful. Moving on to the bathroom separating two of the children's bedrooms, she found nothing in there either. Jared's bathroom required more looking because the drawers were full, but she still came up empty. She lifted the mattress and felt under it as far as her arms could reach, then she picked it up and looked but saw nothing.

How convenient of Jared to tell her to change the sheets —it made this part of her search much easier. Returning briefly to the kitchen, she retrieved a flashlight that she had remembered seeing earlier. Crawling on the floor, she shone the bright light under the bed, under and behind the dresser. Nothing. Then she returned to the children's bedrooms, and searched under the mattresses, and even checked between the sheets on the upper bunks. Behind the dressers and desks also proved futile.

Walking downstairs, she searched between the mattress and the box springs and under and behind the bed. Then after knitting her brow, she opened the nightstand's drawer and pulled out the handcuffs. Holly left the bedroom and looked around the large room. Where would Jared least expect her to go? The heater compartment.

Opening the sliding doors, she found a space toward the back that was invisible if you looked in, and had the added benefit of her being barely able to get her arm into —which meant that Jared could not get his arm in there. She pulled the key from her pocket and put it and the handcuffs into her new hiding place. With the flashlight she could see it, but she hoped that if it came to that, Jared wouldn't think of using one. Shining the light between the heater and water heater, she found nothing of *his* hiding there and nothing resting on the top either. There was nothing of interest in the washer and dryer alcove either.

Frustrated, she pulled the sheets out of the dryer, carried them upstairs, and dumped them on the bed. A thorough search of the kitchen, including looking on top of the cabinets and the top shelves of the pantry revealed nothing at all. There had to be something! She just wasn't finding it. Rummaging through the refrigerator, she found some cheese and made herself a grilled cheese sandwich for lunch. Then she put the clean sheets back on the bed. When it was almost time for Jared to come home, she dug the ovo test from the kitchen drawer to read the instructions.

The first thing she read was to reduce the amount of liquid that you drink two hours before the test, so she immediately got a glass, filled it up with water, and drank it all down. Then she filled it up again and brought it to the table with her.

The way the test worked was to detect the presence of a certain hormone which appeared twenty-four to thirty-six hours before and during "ovo." That made her feel better. It was now the fourth day after her cramp, so she hoped that nothing would show on the test. She had planned to take the test and leave it in the bathroom for Jared to see, but when she learned that you had to read the test within ten minutes or it might show a false positive, she left it in Jared's bathroom so she could take it while he was there. All she needed was for Joseph to jump on a false positive.

Holly drank another glass of water while she waited for Jared to come home. She thought again about Jared leaving the keys in the towel drawer and of how innocent and naive he was. Could she really shoot him if she had to so she could get away? Then she thought of ten men two days a month—twenty gross men grunting and huffing on top of her. And Susan had told her that Joseph had specially picked out the meanest and roughest men in town. Oh, yeah. She could shoot him in a minute.

Just then, the door opened and Jared walked through. "Honey, I'm home!"

At first she just sat there looking at him, but then quickly decided that she better play her part, so she jumped up and hugged him. "Glad to have you home, sweetheart!" She kissed him on the lips.

"You ready to go? Dinner is at five-thirty, and I'd like to get there a little early. He walked into the bedroom without waiting for an answer. "You made the bed up again! Good work, Holly! You're finally coming around! Oh! The ovo test. Did you take it?"

Holly followed him into the bedroom. "Not yet, I wanted to wait for you."

"Well, take it now. Joseph wants a report when we arrive."

"Why? In case it's positive he can take me right there

before dinner?"

Jared shrugged. "It's his right."

"What about *my* rights?"

Jared laughed. "Holly, you know that women have no rights. They're not supposed to. It's men's duty to take care of them. Go on and take the test now."

Holly went into the bathroom, did what she was supposed to do, and flushed the toilet. Then she looked at her watch. Ten minutes and she'd know if she would be violated before dinner. She only felt mildly confident about registering negative. She had never paid any attention before to her own "ovo" and had never needed to. Studying the test strip, she saw one bar prominently displayed and no other. That was a good start at least. After washing her hands, she opened the door. "It will be ready in a few minutes."

"Just take it with us, then. Come on, let's go."

That's exactly what Holly didn't want to happen. She couldn't let Joseph see it after the ten minutes had elapsed. He would find a reason to take her. "No, Jared. I want to wait here until it's finished. It's only a few more minutes."

"We're going now, Holly. Pick it up and let's get going." He walked out of the room.

"I'm not going until it's time to read the test." Holly stayed in the bedroom in front of the bathroom door.

"Holly, get out here right now. I expect you to listen to me when I tell you to do something. This is exactly what Simon was talking about. You are *making* me treat you badly. Now get out here. *Now!*"

She checked her watch. It had been seven minutes. She had to delay three more minutes, so she slipped back into the bathroom, locked the door behind her, and didn't say a word. Jared was still talking in the other room and raising his voice, but she couldn't hear what he was saying, and it didn't matter. What's the worst he could do to her? Beat her? Simon had probably suggested that. Oh, yes, she could definitely shoot him.

With one minute to go, he tried the bathroom door and found it locked. Then he hit it with his hand. "Holly, get your butt out here right now, or when you do I'm going to have to hit you! You're not giving me a choice!"

"So I should come out and be willing to get hit, Jared? I don't think so."

"Holly, you have one minute to get out of there and then I'm going to find the key or break the door down! Then you'll really be in for it."

She didn't need a minute, she only needed twenty seconds, so she slowly unlocked the door and opened it. "Okay, the test finished, Jared. Only one line. I'm not ovo." After he glanced at it, she picked it up, squished it in her hand the best she could and followed him to the kitchen. Then she opened the compartment where the garbage was and moved it around in the coffee grounds. Before she had a chance to wash her hands again, Jared grabbed one of them and pulled her bodily out of the house.

As they drove the short distance to Joseph's, Jared stayed silent until they pulled up in front of the house—

white with green shutters, exactly like theirs. Then he turned his head to glare at her. "I am so angry at you right now, Holly, that I'm half tempted to tell Joseph that the test was positive."

Bile came up suddenly in Holly's throat, and she forced it down. She turned her head, narrowed her eyes, and slowly enunciated each word as she spoke. "And I can tell you this, Jared Tanner, if you do that, I will kill you."

CHAPTER THIRTY-SEVEN

OLIVIA HAD LISTENED to the conversation between Buck and Darryl with the discerning mind of a writer. So Buck, jerk that he was, had a redeeming quality after all. He didn't say the word, but it was obvious that he thought Carter was a pedophile. She couldn't have written his character any better if she had tried. It was perfect. And she had learned something else. The Messianic Privilege was real.

There had been rumors about it, but she hadn't read about any hard evidence that proved it to be true. She didn't suppose, however, that Carter had broadened the privilege to extend to anyone else. It had been a point of contention after Dean read the book. He had said that during her research—which they shared and talked about each night—she had found that gurus or messiahs don't have any friends. Therefore, Simon Banks would never have extended the Messianic Privilege to Joseph. Olivia had smiled at Dean and shrugged her shoulders.

"Literary *privilege*. It makes for a better story and more tension at the end." Messianic Privilege. That didn't bode well for her in Plenty. Carter could do what he wanted with her whenever he wanted. And there was nothing Dean could do about it.

She shook her head. Why oh why had she told Dean not to call? If she hadn't told him that, then maybe he would be on their trail by now. And why did he have to work two shifts? If he hadn't, at least he would only be a few hours behind. Olivia slumped in the seat and shook her head. She would be in Plenty almost before Dean even knew she was missing. There may not be anything left of her by the time Dean arrived to save her. His rescue attempt would all be for naught. Darryl's voice interrupted her thoughts.

"Buck, get off the freeway and pull over. I have to take a piss."

"You shoulda done that when we stopped for gas." A slight smile shone on Buck's face as he said the words.

"C'mon, Buck. Don't fuck with me. I've got to go."

"You should have thought about that before." Buck shook his head. "I'm not stopping."

Olivia could hear Darryl unhooking his belt. "Fine. I'll just piss on the floor right here. Don't worry, I won't get any on your shoes."

Buck stepped on the brake, throwing Darryl forward in his seatbelt, and throwing Olivia—who had never fastened hers —against the front seat. "I'll get off at the next exit. Put that thing away," Buck grumbled. Then as he pulled off the freeway, he brightened. "Oh! How lucky. There's a gas station right up there."

"No, Buck. Pull over on that street there. By the vacant lot. I'm not leaving this truck again."

"Fine!" Buck jerked the wheel and the truck hit the curb.

Darryl started getting out of the truck, but before he had both legs out, he turned back to Buck and grabbed the bag with the gun in it.

"Hey, what are you doing with that?" asked Buck indignantly.

"Insurance, Buck. I don't want you driving off with our precious cargo." Darryl took a step away from the truck, still hidden by the door. Then he proceeded to relieve himself. After he zipped up, he opened the back door. "You gotta go?"

Olivia nodded.

"Then get out here and give me your hands."

"You're not going to un-cuff her, are you? That would be stupid. She already moved the cuffs around from behind her back," Buck called through the door.

"It's not like we're not fast enough to catch her if she runs, Buck, but no, I'm not." He took off Olivia's left handcuff and reattached it to the truck's front armrest. "You'll have to do the best you can with one hand."

Olivia looked at him and over her shoulder at Buck who stared at her. Nothing like a little privacy so a girl could go. But she had to go so bad that she could have gone in front of a whole auditorium full of people. With her free hand, she reached under her skirt and pulled down her underwear. Then she squatted down next to the truck and picked up the back of her skirt just enough for it not to get wet, but not enough so Buck could even catch a glimpse of her bare flesh. Better not to tempt him any more than she had to.

When she finished getting herself back together, she stood up and thanked Darryl as he reattached the handcuffs and shoved her into the backseat. Although she didn't expect a "you're welcome," she didn't think he would do that, so she went sprawling onto the seat and had barely pulled her feet in when he slammed the door. Olivia sighed and curled back into the corner of the backseat. She closed her eyes to block out the situation she was in if only for a minute. But the emotional day and the movement of the truck lulled her to sleep. Later, when the truck swerved off the interstate, Olivia awoke and was shocked to see the sign that said, "Entering Plenty, Texas." Oh, no, she thought.

CHAPTER THIRTY-EIGHT

Family Dinner

JARED STEPPED OUT of the truck, met her at the front, and took her hand. "I don't want Joseph to know we were fighting." They walked up to the door, Jared knocked twice, and without waiting for an answer, opened the door and walked in. Entering the kitchen, Holly saw an exact duplicate of their kitchen, right down to the yellow hen clock on the wall. Susan was at the oven, Marina at the refrigerator.

Joseph walked in from the other room. "Hmmm. You're holding hands, but you both look fit to be tied." He laughed. "Have we had our first marriage fight?" he asked in a baby voice.

Holly pulled her hand away from Jared's and said, "He hit me. But I've learned my lesson now." Then she turned away from Jared and walked up to Susan. "Can I help you?"

From her peripheral vision, she saw Joseph slap Jared on the shoulder. "Good going, little bro! You're listening to Simon! This might work out after all."

Then he whispered something in Jared's ear, but all Holly could hear was "positive?" She knew exactly what he was referring to. Jared shook his head and said, "Shhhh," and they walked into the dining room and sat at the table.

"No, we're good here, Holly. Why don't you go ahead and sit at the table"—Susan nodded to the small wooden kitchen table—"and we'll serve you as soon as we finish serving the men."

"What?" said Holly.

Marina put her hand on Holly's arm and pulled out a chair at the kitchen table for her. "Here, Holly," she whispered. "Sit here."

"I'd rather help!" said Holly forcefully.

Susan turned from pulling something out of the oven and said quietly, "I don't think it's a good idea, Holly. We'll talk later. Trust me."

The last time Susan had said that to her she had told Holly the truth, but Holly hadn't believed her. So she nodded and sat down at the table with her back to the men. After several trips to the men's table, Susan and Marina brought Holly a plate of food and carried their own plates to the table with her.

"Sorry, it's like this, Holly." Susan put her napkin in her lap and picked up her fork. "But the platters are over there. It's the only way I could do it."

Marina leaned forward. "Did Jared really *hit* you?"

"Shhh!" Susan looked at her sternly. "We'll talk later."

Holly looked at Marina and moved her head from side to side almost imperceptibly. "Thank you for inviting us to dinner, Susan. It looks delicious." She could barely hear the men's conversation, but from what she *could* hear it was about Simon's sermon, the wedding, and the gas station. So she knew that they could hear anything that she said here at the table as well.

"It was so you could get your wedding gifts! Are you excited to see them? You got some really good stuff!" Marina smiled at her with bright eyes.

Holly was about to ask how Marina knew when Susan shook her head gently and mouthed the word "Later." So Holly nodded and said, "Yes, I'm eager to see them!" She tried to sound enthusiastic, but thought her voice sounded disgusted instead. Maybe not, though, because Susan didn't scowl at her.

"Do you want to know what some of them were?" asked Marina.

"Marina, no," said Susan quietly. "So how did cleanup go last night, Holly? I should have told you about that, but it never even dawned on me that you wouldn't know about it."

Holly, trying to sound nonchalant, said, "Oh, it went fine. I wish I had known about it, because then I could have brought other shoes to wear."

"Oh, that's not allowed," said Marina. "You have to wear

all of your wedding clothes, including your shoes. It teaches us to be able to clean anywhere, anytime, and to be careful while we do it."

Holly nodded while she cut off a piece of pork chop. "Sounds like a valuable thing to learn." She didn't look up when she said it, because she knew that at least Susan would probably be looking at her in disbelief.

They finished the rest of their dinner talking about nonessential, mundane topics, which suited Holly perfectly. Afterward, they cleared the dishes off the table and then cleared the dishes for the men. When they started washing the dishes, Joseph spoke up. "Susan, you can do the dishes later. Take Marina and Holly downstairs so we men can talk business."

Holly thought, yeah, right, business, but she didn't say anything. Susan said, "All right," and then she finished putting the leftovers away. "Let's go, girls," and she led the way through the living room that looked exactly like Jared's and down into the basement that was also exactly like Jared's. She closed the door behind them.

Holly glanced over at the heater compartment and then looked at Marina, who shook her head. With a frustrated look on her face, she walked over there and silently pleaded with Marina, who shook her head again.

Susan stood there with her hands on her hips. "Why do you two have such funny looks on your faces?" Then she noticed where Holly was standing. "Oh! Marina! Do you really think that I don't know about your little *secret*? Go ahead! Open it up for Holly!"

Holly didn't wait another second, she opened the sliding doors and slowly pulled the cord—in case it might make a noise as it opened—and stood there listening.

"Shhh. Is the door closed yet?" It was Jared.

"Yes, little brother, the door is closed. So was it positive or not?"

"Not."

"You wouldn't lie to me, would you now? I'd only have to wait another month, and if I found out you were lying—" Joseph didn't finish his sentence, but Holly could feel the tension in his voice.

"No, Joseph, I'm not lying. Holly is not thrilled with the idea of—"

"She needs to learn to submit, Jared. None of them are thrilled in the beginning. But they get used to it, and I know they start to like it. You'll see. She'll look forward to it after a while."

Jared made a noise that wasn't quite a laugh. "Yeah, well I know what you have planned for her—the roughest men in town—and I can guarantee you that she won't look forward to that. I have half a mind, Joseph, to still claim First Rites. It's not too late, you know."

Oh, Jared, thought Holly, you can be sweet. Marina raised her eyebrows and Susan, who was standing right there too, nodded her head.

"If you do that, little brother, I will invoke the Messianic Privilege, and I'll have her anyway. As much as I want. Any time I want. I won't have to wait for *ovo*."

Holly suddenly felt sick to her stomach. The blood rushed to her head, and her feet were unsteady beneath her. She would have fallen over—against the heater—if it hadn't been for Marina and Susan supporting her.

"Messianic Privilege? Sounds like it's for Simon only."

"It's Simon's latest revelation, and he said that he would word it in a way that it would include me."

"Okay, okay! I won't claim First Rites, but I would really appreciate it if you would see your way to change the men on the schedule."

"Trust me, little bro. It will be good for her. And if she handles it well, I'll change it for the next one. Anyway, three appointments tomorrow with those three hot blondes! How about that, hey? Which one—"

Susan leaned forward and whispered quietly to Holly, "They're finished talking about that now. They'll spend the rest of the evening talking about women. Come on, let me help you to the chair."

While Susan walked Holly to the chair, Marina quietly closed the vent and the sliding doors leading to the heater. Holly sat there for a few minutes with her head in her hands. Susan and Marina stayed silent until she picked up her head again.

She looked from one to the other. "I've got to get out of here. I really do."

"I know," said Susan.

CHAPTER THIRTY-NINE

WHEN OLIVIA SAW the sign "Entering Plenty, Texas" she remembered back to when she and Dean had driven through, and she had turned on the remote cameras as they passed the sign. It was so long ago—before she had written the book—but seemed more recent. Would she still have written the book had she known this would happen? Shrugging her shoulders, she thought she could have used a pen name. It would have taken them longer to find her, but they probably would have eventually. Pen names weren't as sacrosanct as people imagined. But, no, she wasn't the pen name type. So the answer was yes, she still would have written the book. And if she could possibly get safely out of here with her body and mind still intact, maybe she would write a nonfiction book on what had happened to her after being kidnapped. It should make interesting reading for the uninitiated.

As they drove by the light from the gas station, Olivia checked her watch. Ten o'clock. Dean wouldn't even be getting off work for another hour. What a fool she'd been not to listen to his warnings. Now, unfortunately, she would pay the price. And that price could be fatal.

A few minutes later, they drove into the big gold church's parking lot. There was only one other car there in a space marked "Messiah." Of course Carter must live at the church. Where else would a messiah live?

Buck stopped the truck. "Let's get this over with."

Darryl stepped out of the truck and opened the back door. "Get out. Now you'll get what's coming to you!" He grabbed her by the handcuffs, and when she faltered and almost fell, he hauled her up, tightening the cuffs and hurting her wrists.

"Ouch!"

"Shut up and let's go." Darryl pushed her in front of him, and the three of them walked into the back door of the church.

Carter's office door was open, and they walked inside. "Carter? We're back and we have your prisoner." No answer. "Where do you think he is?" asked Darryl.

Buck scowled and said under his breath, "Idiot." He walked forward to a door at the back of the office marked *Messiah's Private Sanctuary. Do not disturb!!* and he pounded on it with both fists. "Carter! We're back! Carter!"

The door swung open with such force that it almost hit Buck. "How *dare* you disturb me in my private chamber!" His face was bright red with rage and spittle flew out of his mouth. Darryl stood back with his hands in front of him as if to say, it was him, not me. Buck just listened as Carter raged on, but his hands were still in fists, and Olivia could tell that he wasn't taking the berating well. "You interrupted me in the middle of a revelation! How *dare* you! It may take me *days* to get it back, and I need it by tomorrow!" He grabbed Buck by the front of his shirt and came within an inch of his face. "If I don't get that revelation finished by tomorrow, you're in *big* trouble. You hear me?" Buck's fist started to raise up, but then Carter released him, and the hand dropped back down.

"Fine! What do you want us to do with *her*?" Buck asked.

"*That's* what I was trying to find out when you busted in here!" Carter stepped back into his sanctuary, but before closing the door, he turned back to them. "Just get her out of here." Carter shook. "Her very presence makes me uncomfortable. Take her to the jail for safekeeping."

"Come on, Buck, let's go." Darryl pulled Olivia by the arm.

Buck started to follow and then caught Carter before he closed the sanctuary door. "Carter, can we procreate with her?"

Olivia's eyes opened wide and her heart started beating wildly while she waited for Carter to answer. He stood there lost in thought. "Yeah, why not. You got her here in one piece. As long as she's ovo, procreate all you want. Just don't mess her up, any." He glanced at Darryl. "You can procreate, too, Darryl. As long as she's ovo."

"How do we know?" asked Buck.

"There's a test kit in the top right hand drawer of my desk. Now leave me alone." And Carter slammed the door behind him.

CHAPTER FORTY

Girl Talk

HOLLY HADN'T WANTED to say anything like that in front of Susan, but she couldn't help herself. Now she was glad she did. She finally had some validation, but she never expected it from Susan. "Really? You know?"

Susan nodded. "This isn't the place for you."

"What changed your mind?" Holly glanced up and noticed the black cat clock above the stairs, something else exactly like Jared's.

"Because I told her what you said about gang bang and that God really does like women," Marina said.

Susan nodded. "I always had a feeling that we weren't hearing the whole story. Ever since I was forced to marry Joseph—not to mention everything he's done to me—I've had my doubts." She raised her eyebrows to Holly. "But no one to voice them to until now. So I want to thank you for that."

Holly smiled. "You're welcome." Then Holly noticed an old cast iron frying pan and a sauce pan with a chip in the handle. "What are these?"

"Your wedding gifts!" Marina said.

"You mean here they give people *used* gifts?" She reached for the handle of the frying pan, found it sticky, grimaced, and wiped her hand on her skirt.

"Ah, Joseph," said Susan. "He still thinks Jared owes him for *detaining* you here, so he decided that *he* would open the gifts and take what he wanted first. I'd been on him to get me a new frying pan and some other stuff, so he just took them and replaced them with our old ones. If you don't want the stuff, leave it here and I'll get rid of it."

"I should probably bring it back to Jared's so he can decide. You know how *these* men are!" The three women laughed which made Holly feel good. "Is there anything new?"

"Yeah! Lots! Come in and look in my bedroom." Marina stood up and walked over there.

"You sleep down here? Why not upstairs in one of those other bedrooms?"

Marina put her hands on her hips. "Because Joseph says I talk too much and until I'm a woman who's doing her part to grow Children of the Light with babies, I will stay down here."

Holly winced and looked at Susan. "That's an insult to you. Does he say it in front of you?"

"All the time." She nodded. "All the time. Any chance he

gets to remind me that I'm not doing my part, he takes advantage of."

"What a jerk." Holly looked at the boxes on the bed. There were can openers, crock pots, blenders, and a set of dishes for eight. When her eyes got to a set of silverware, she picked it up. "Joseph didn't want these? They look really nice."

"He took a much better set and took the good blender too," Marina said.

"It was a food processor," said Susan. "A nice one. I'm sorry, Holly."

She leaned forward and whispered, "I'm not going to need them where I'm going, so it's good that you can get good use out of them. Besides, it's not your fault, Susan. He did it, not you."

"Yeah, but I married him."

Holly shook her head. "It wasn't your choice. You have nothing to be sorry for."

"Derek wanted me to leave, and I wouldn't. I was afraid that I wouldn't go to the Promised Land if I followed him out of here." She turned away and sniffled. "If I had, he'd be alive right now."

Marina turned to her and put a hand on her arm. "You don't know for sure he's dead, Susan."

Nodding to the sliding doors of the heater compartment, Susan said, "Yes, I do. I overheard Joseph and Simon talking."

"I'm sorry, Susan. I'm so sorry," said Holly.

Susan turned around and stepped back toward the bed. "Let's get this all packaged up before Jared's ready to leave."

Before they began, Holly looked around at the room that was exactly like the one where she had been held captive. "Why is this house and our house exactly the same?"

"All the houses and all the furnishings in the houses of the Children of the Light community are exactly the same. That way nobody can be jealous of anybody else," said Marina.

Holly nodded. It was just another thing added to the rest of the weirdnesses of the group. While the three women packed the gifts in the boxes that Joseph had brought in for them, she said, "By the way, Susan, I owe you an apology."

"Why?" she asked.

"You were right about First Rites, Jared procreating after we married, *and* them taking the gas out of my gas tank. I'm sorry I didn't believe you."

"Ah, no big deal," said Susan without looking up.

"So did you hear what happened this morning?" Holly asked.

Both Susan and Marina looked up and said in unison, "No."

"Joseph and Jared set me up to see if I would leave. Jared hid my car key where he knew I'd find it, and Joseph had men stationed at each end of the street to catch me in case I ran."

"What did you do?" asked Marina.

Holly told them what happened, and as they laughed about it, they pushed and pulled the big boxes out to the main room, and then they sat at the table.

Susan looked at Holly with a wry smile. "So how was your wedding night?"

"You mean aside from the cleanup?" Holly asked.

"Yeah. The other part of it," Susan said.

"I didn't want to because I felt exhausted from the cleanup. But Jared insisted that we had to consummate the marriage that night."

"That's because the marriage isn't official if it isn't consummated the same night as the wedding," said Marina.

"Well, it was over in just a few minutes, which surprised me. So, I tried again in the morning, expecting, you know, *more*."

"But you didn't get more, did you?" asked Susan.

"No. What's up with that?" Holly asked.

"The men here are all used to *procreating* with many different women in a month. And since women don't matter and are only vehicles to bring more children into the world, all they care about is their own pleasure. Women don't like sex, anyway."

"Not like that, we don't!" said Holly, which made everyone laugh again.

"Not to change the subject or anything, but what are you going to do, Holly?" Susan said in a quiet voice even though the basement door was shut tight.

"I've already started to look for something I can use for

my escape." She looked down and then looked straight at each woman. "And I realize now that the *something* that I'm looking for is a gun."

"Have you found it?" Marina asked.

Holly frowned and shook her head. "No luck at all."

"Joseph gave him one last Christmas, so I know he has one. It's just like Joseph's," said Marina.

"I don't know where it would be, and I searched everywhere! But if you're sure he has one, I can search again."

"I might know where it is. Follow me." Susan stood up and walked back to the bedroom. Leaning over the back of the bed, she pulled the sailboat picture off the wall. Behind it was a safe.

"Wow!" said Marina. "I've slept in here for years, and I didn't know that was there!"

Susan put her finger to her lips, replaced the picture, and the three women returned to the table. "I could bet it was there." She lowered her voice. "And I'd also bet that the combination will be Jared's birthday."

"Which is?" asked Holly.

"January 12, 1990."

"Thank you, Susan. I can't thank you enough."

"My revenge. On Joseph *and* on Simon."

"What do you mean?" asked Holly.

"Simon told Joseph not to let you get away, because he wanted you and he intended to have you."

"Oh, great," said Holly. "I have an admirer."

"I heard Joseph going on and on about your ovo. It was

negative, I expect," said Susan.

"Thankfully," said Holly.

"When do you think it's going to be?" asked Marina.

"Only a guess, but I think I just had it. So I'm safe for a while."

"Let's hope so," said Susan. "You heard what Joseph said about the Messianic Privilege. As soon as Simon makes that official, Joseph can use it on you. Luckily, Simon is busy right now with the new town that he's building. That's why he couldn't stay any longer."

Holly looked at Susan and tilted her head. "I still don't understand why you want to get revenge on Simon."

Without answering Holly, Susan looked at Marina. "I'm sorry you have to hear this, Marina." Then Susan looked back at Holly. "Because it was Simon's idea that I walk down the aisle on my hands and knees. Joseph readily agreed—but it was Simon's idea." Looking back at Marina, she said, "I'm sorry to disillusion you, Marina."

Marina shrugged. "I was disillusioned when he slapped Holly in front of the whole congregation. Women may be chattel, but that was uncalled for."

The basement door opened, and Jared poked his head in. "Holly, let's go home now."

"Can you and Joseph come help us carry the boxes up? They're heavy," said Holly.

"Sure," Jared said and started down the stairs.

"No!" Joseph's voice boomed out. "You three can bring them up here by yourselves. And hurry up about it. I want to go to bed! Jared, get back up here. The *women* can do it."

CHAPTER FORTY-ONE

WHEN THEY HAD climbed back into the truck, Buck looked at Darryl and grinned. "See? You protected her for no reason. Carter said we could fuck her after all."

Olivia sat in the back shaking, but Buck's use of procreate in front of Carter and fuck in front of Darryl fascinated her. In spite of himself and contrary to what he claimed, he must have had some respect for Carter—or else he didn't want to provoke any more of Carter's wrath.

"No, he did not say that. He said we could *procreate* with her *if* she was ovo."

Buck looked at Darryl with a pitying expression on his face and then started the truck. "And how is Carter gonna know, smart guy?"

Darryl held up the ovulation test strip in his hand. "If she's ovo, we'll show it to Carter."

"Carter didn't ask us to do that!"

"I know it's what he'd want. And that's that, Buck. We're not procreating unless she's ovo." He crossed his arms in front of him. "*You* might still be in big trouble if he can't get his revelation back before tomorrow."

"What's so important about tomorrow, anyway?"

"Dude, it's Sunday. He wants to announce in front of everyone what he plans to do with *her*."

Olivia didn't have time to worry about whether she was ovo or not. The jail was just a minute or two from the church. When she had done her research, she had discovered that *most women* ovulate sometime after their period. The qualifier being most women. But since hers were always on time, she hoped that since it was a few days *before* her period, she would be safe. She also hoped she was right *and* that Buck would listen to Darryl. Luckily, Darryl had only picked up a single test strip instead of the package. Because if they had the package they'd know that the results might show a false positive after more than ten minutes. And if Buck had read the package and not Darryl, it would be even worse— he'd want to wait more than ten minutes.

When the truck stopped, Darryl hauled her back out again and shoved her toward the door of the sheriff's office. When they walked inside, no one was there, but the light was on. Darryl handed her the test strip and gave her another shove toward a door on the opposite side of the room than Olivia had imagined it. "Take this and go in there!"

"Wait a minute! What if she does it wrong so it shows up negative?" asked Buck.

"I read the instructions. There is a *control* part. If she doesn't do it right, then the control part will look odd. I'll know."

"All right," scowled Buck.

"Would you undo these, please?" Olivia held out her handcuffed hands.

"No way!" Buck raised his voice. "Don't do it, Darryl."

"There's no window in the bathroom, is there?" Olivia asked.

"Shut up!" Buck pushed her shoulder knocking her off balance.

"Ah, she's right, Buck. Stand by the front door. She's not getting past you. And if she runs that way"—he nodded to a partway-open door on the other side of the room—"she'll go into the cells. She's not going anywhere."

Darryl unlocked the cuffs, and Olivia rubbed her wrists. Then she took the test strip, walked into the bathroom, and closed and locked the door. She took her time, peed on the strip, washed her hands, and used her clean hand to take a long drink of water. They had given her no water since they kidnapped her more than eleven hours before. When she finished drinking, she forced down some more to make sure she wasn't too dehydrated. Then, anticipating no toilet paper in the cell, she took a good long strip of it, folded it neatly, and tucked it into her skirt pocket. She had glanced into the mirror briefly, but the image that stared back at her was so unkempt that she didn't want to look again.

As she was about to unlock and open the door, Buck pounded on it and tried the lock. "Hey, she locked it! Open up in there! What are you doing?"

Olivia opened the door and narrowed her eyes at him. "Chill, boy. I'm not going anywhere." She handed him the test strip.

"Here, Darryl. You read the instructions. Is she ovo?"

Darryl looked at it and held it under the desk lamp. "It doesn't look like it, but the package said that it takes a few minutes to be sure."

"It takes seven minutes," said Olivia, giving herself and the test some leeway.

"Shut up!" screamed Buck.

"Oh, she's right," said Darryl. "How long has it been?"

"Five minutes. Is it going toward the positive side?" asked Buck hopefully.

"Naw. It's negative, Buck. Sorry." He looked up at Buck and shrugged.

"Oh, come on, Darryl. Carter doesn't have to know!"

"No, Buck. Absolutely not. Carter said we could *if* she was ovo. She's *not*. Discussion over."

"Fine, just fine, Darryl. You obey Carter like a little lamb going to slaughter. I'm my own man!" Buck sat down at the desk and crossed his arms. "I'll stay here and keep an eye on her."

Darryl laughed. "Yeah, right, Buck. Either we both stay or I stay alone. You choose."

Buck stood up and shook his finger in Darryl's face. "I *hate* Carter! I hate that he thinks he can yell at me and treat me like that! He's a lunatic and a pedophile!"

"Get out, Buck! Get out of here and never come back, or I'm going to tell Carter what you said! Get out!" Darryl pointed toward the door.

Buck took two quick strides to the door, opened it, walked through, and slammed it behind him. A second later, he stormed back inside. In a calm voice that was shaky with emotion, Buck said, "I'll tell you this, Darryl. I hate Carter and I'm going to *kill* him!"

"You're always making empty threats, Buck. You're just a

big blowhard! Now leave me alone and get out of here!"

Buck stepped through the door slamming it again; and Olivia heard his truck drive away. Darryl took her by the arm and led her into where the cells were. He opened the first one up, shoved her inside, and locked the door.

"Thank you for not leaving me here with him."

"I didn't do it for you. I did it for me. If I let him do something that goes against what Carter says, then I'm just as guilty as he is, and I won't go to the Promised Land." Then he walked through the doorway back into the office and closed the door.

CHAPTER FORTY-TWO

A Sailing We Will Go

As THEY WERE driving home, with Holly still huffing from the strain of pushing and pulling the boxes upstairs, Jared spoke first. "You know, I told Joseph that I was thinking of still claiming First Rites, but it didn't work out."

Holly's first impulse was to say "Yeah, I'll bet," but she held her tongue and instead said, "I appreciate that, Jared."

"Why did you tell Joseph that I hit you?" Jared wondered.

"Because I knew that he'd like that. Did you confess that you really hadn't?"

"No, but I feel bad that I lied to him. I never have before."

"You didn't. I did. Nothing to feel bad about."

"Here we are." Jared shut off the engine, got out of the truck, and walked to the door.

Holly changed into her nightgown and crawled into bed,

not knowing what to expect. Jared crawled in next to her and before he turned off the bedside light, he said, "I know you want to please me, Holly, but I have three appointments tomorrow so I need my rest."

She didn't answer, but turned away, not disappointed at all. His idea of making love wasn't even enough to get her started. And right now, since her decision to leave, she wasn't interested anyway. All she could think of was how soon Jared would leave in the morning so she could look behind the sailboat picture. If there was a gun behind it—it would be her key out of there. That reminded her: if she was going to use those handcuffs that she hid away downstairs, she would need to find his key. She hoped it was on his keyring.

The next morning when Jared climbed out of bed to take his shower, Holly pretended she was still sleeping. When she heard the shower door close, she jumped up to rifle through his jeans. The keys were there, including one very small one that had to be the handcuff key. She slipped it off the keyring, replaced the keys into his jeans, and pushed the handcuff key far under the mattress for safekeeping. Then she climbed back into bed.

Jared came out of the bathroom drying his head. "Hi, sleepyhead! Did you sleep well?"

"Yup." Holly yawned as if she had just awakened.

"You need to take the ovo test again today. Every day from now on, all right?"

"I'll take it right now, then." She swung her legs over the

side of the bed and stretched.

"Hurry up. I need to leave early. You don't have to make breakfast today."

"You'll go without eating?" She wrapped her arms around him and gazed up into his face with feigned concern. "That's not good."

"I'll eat donuts and be fine. I have to get to the station before my appointments. Now go on, take your test. I have to leave." He pulled away from her and gave her a swat on her behind.

She walked away several paces, turned back, and looked at him seductively. "Are you sure you don't want to stay home for a while . . . ?"

"Go on, Holly. You know what I have to do today!"

She walked into the bathroom and slammed the door. A few minutes later, she came out. Jared was already in the kitchen, so she dressed and walked out there.

"I know you want to please me, Holly, but I have other matters to attend to. You know that."

Holly nodded but didn't look at him. That's exactly what she wanted him to think—that she wanted to "please" him. Disgusting.

"I'll see you later." He put his hand on the door.

"No, Jared, no! Wait for the test so you can see the results." She glanced at her watch. The test needed four more minutes.

"You can just tell me. No big deal. I trust you." He turned the handle.

"Yes, but Joseph won't. And if he asks, I want you to be able to tell him the truth: that you saw the test and it was negative." She turned to walk back into the bathroom. "It's done now. Let me show you and then you can leave."

It still had one minute to go, but he wouldn't know that. She picked it up and brought it into the kitchen to show him. Glancing at her watch, she said, "Ten minutes on the nose. Here, take a look. Only one line. Negative."

"Got it! Bye!" And he walked out the door.

Holly pressed her face against the glass and watched as the truck pulled away and disappeared out of view. She shook her head and thought about how grateful she would be to get out of this place for good. After throwing the test in the garbage, she washed her hands, made coffee, and started some oatmeal. When it and the coffee were done, she sat at the table to eat. Taking her time, she tried to relax, although every muscle in her body was aiming toward the basement steps so she could see if the gun was in the safe. But she wanted to make sure that Jared *and* Joseph were occupied with their *appointments* before she started.

Half an hour later, after Holly had washed the coffee pot and the dishes, dried them, and put them away, she opened the door and glanced out. His truck was gone from the station. It was time.

First she put her hand under the mattress in the bedroom to get the handcuff key, and then she stuck it in the pocket of her skirt. Trying to contain her excitement, she walked carefully down the basement stairs. All she needed was to fall headlong down them, and then she'd never get out of here. When she reached the bottom, she ran to the bedroom and lifted the sailboat picture gently off the wall. Sure enough, right behind it was the safe.

Before she touched the dial, she checked to see what number it was on. Zero. She pulled the handle, but it didn't budge. That would have been too good to hope for. Turning the dial to the right several times to clear it, she could feel her excitement building inside. Then she turned it right to one, then left to twelve, then right to ninety. Although she didn't hear any click, maybe this safe didn't make a sound like that. Pulling the handle, she was devastated when it didn't budge. It was the wrong combination! Now what would she do?

Holly sat on the bed and fought off the tears that threatened to come into her eyes. She couldn't allow herself to feel defeated. If she gave up hope, then she'd never get out of here, and she would be entertaining Joseph and eighteen other men every month. An idea occurred to her, and she stood up to try it.

Turning the dial *left* this time to clear it, she put the combination in again, but started with the left. She felt the click rather than heard it, and when she pulled the handle, it opened. Putting her hand in and feeling around, she felt the gun, a clip, and some papers underneath it. When she pulled out the gun and the clip, she smiled. It was a gun exactly like the one her boyfriend in college had when he made her go shooting with him. Checking the clip, she saw that it was empty, and looking into the chamber, she saw there were no bullets in there either. Great. She had a gun, knew how to use it, but didn't have any bullets. That would do her a lot of good. Jared would know there were no bullets for the gun, so she couldn't even threaten him with it.

She put the gun and the clip back in the safe on top of the papers. Then she closed the door, turned the dial a few times, and let it rest back on zero where she had found it. At least she had discovered where the gun was. Maybe Susan or Marina would know where he kept the bullets. She could at least hope for that.

With the sailboat picture in her hands, she was about to replace it when she heard the front door open and footsteps in the kitchen. Holly put the picture back on the wall as fast as she could, being careful to straighten it before she walked away.

CHAPTER FORTY-THREE

WHEN DEAN DROVE by the Plenty, Texas, freeway exit, it was all he could do to keep himself from storming in there and trying to rescue Olivia by himself. But he realized that if he did that, he would probably end up getting both of them killed. So he drove straight past it for a few more minutes until he reached the exit that Carlos had told him to take when they spoke an hour before. He coasted off the freeway, drove a quarter of a mile, and pulled into the Denny's parking lot. There were a lot of cars there for three in the morning.

When he walked inside to look for Carlos, he found him sitting with five other men at a big, round table toward the back of the restaurant. Six men plus himself! Dean thought they might have a chance. He walked in and smiled when he saw who the men were. All but one of them were men he had worked with in the Rangers.

"Carlos, thank you!"

The men stood up when they heard Dean's voice, and Dean shook their hands one by one. "You guys don't have to do this. It's going to be dangerous and risky."

"Just shut up, Dean," Paul Milton joked. "We all know that

you'd do it for us in a heartbeat!" Paul was only five-eight, but he was stocky and all muscle. He could take down a grizzly bear.

"I'm so sorry about Olivia. We'll get her." Cole Branson was black, tall, mean on the outside, and gentle as a puppy dog on the inside. Dean thought he might be here. It had been Cole's shift that he had taken the night he was on security duty, and Cole had felt guilty about it ever since. But Dean had said Cole would have done the same thing, and since Cole had a wife and family, it was better that it happened to Dean and not him. Cole still felt bad.

David Alexander shook his hand next. David was tall, tough, and gay. He was the best sharpshooter of the bunch, and Dean was glad that he had come.

Jamie Bolt had a handlebar mustache and longish blonde hair, and he always had a smile on his face. "Don't worry, Dean. We'll get her out safely."

These were all men Dean had worked with in the Rangers. They all respected him and were here willing to risk their lives and their livelihoods to help him. As emotionally jacked up as Dean was, he almost started bawling right there. Then the sixth man came out from behind Dean's friends, and Dean recognized him immediately. He was the older cowboy who had come to Olivia's book signing and had warned them.

"I'm John Hauser, Dean. I'm sorry that this happened to your woman. I tried to warn you."

"Hello, John. Thank you for coming." Dean shook his hand. "I tried to warn her, too, but she was too pigheaded to listen. I'm hoping that her pigheadedness hasn't gotten her killed already."

"I'm glad to be here to help you, and I'm hoping we can get my daughter out at the same time—if she's still alive."

Dean looked him straight in the eye. "Let's hope they're *both* still alive, John."

The men sat down at the table and started discussing the situation. Dean looked at the clock on the wall. "How soon do you think we can go in?"

"I know you want to go in as soon as possible, Dean, but it's not prudent to do it that way. We will have the best possible outcome if we wait until morning when they're all in church." Carlos patted Dean's hand. "I know it's a crapshoot and the guy is crazy, but I don't think he'll kill her right away." Thoughts of what he *would* do to her hung in the air. "Let's hope not, anyway."

Dean looked down and nodded. "So have you guys all been discussing it already? I trust you. What do you have in mind?"

"Their church service starts at ten o'clock. *Everyone* is at church. It's mandatory, so there are no guards at the edge of town." Carlos looked around at Dean, and Dean nodded his head again.

"I sure wish I had known that before," said John Hauser. "I might have been able to get my daughter out of there before now."

"One man with all those cultists, John, you still wouldn't have stood a chance," said David.

The discussion went on with Dean drifting in and out of focus. Olivia in there with those crazies for seven more hours. Even if they didn't kill her—the possibilities were too horrible to think about. And knowing how tough Olivia thought she was, who knew what she could provoke them to do to her? But the plan that the men discussed sounded logical and doable. Cole had even google-earthed the church for more information. They were as prepared as they could possibly be. It was a good rescue plan, and Dean only hoped that Olivia was still alive to be rescued.

CHAPTER FORTY-FOUR

Women Are Afraid of the Dark!

As HOLLY WALKED up the stairs, she heard someone say, "Holly! Holly!" in a quiet voice. It was Marina. Holly felt so relieved, she almost missed a stair and went a tumbling.

"Marina! I'm on my way up." Holly reached the top of the stairs to see Marina, flushed with excitement, waiting for her there. "What are you doing here? Where's Susan?"

"Susan's at home, where *I* should be! I snuck out while Joseph had his appointments." She took a few deep breaths and sank into the couch. "I ran all the way here—the back way, so it took longer."

Holly sat down across from her. "What's up? Why are you here?"

"Susan wanted to know if you found the gun," Marina said, still trying to catch her breath.

"Yes, I did, but unfortunately there were no bullets. And I can't even threaten Jared with an unloaded gun, because he would know there were no bullets for it."

"Oh." Marina looked disappointed. "That is bad. Well, we'll figure out something! Don't worry!"

Holly nodded her head. "I *am* worried. How am I going to get out of here? All I have to help me right now is one set of handcuffs. And how would I even get them on him?" She looked down. "I'm starting to get *really* worried."

"Listen, Susan wanted me to tell you that we're doing our grocery shopping tomorrow, and that you should ask Jared if you could go with us."

"Oh! That's a great idea! I do need to get some more food to cook. Oh, wait. I don't need food to cook if I'm leaving."

"You need Jared to think you're staying. Susan says that if he gets any hint of you still wanting to leave, he'll tell Joseph, and then you *will* be in trouble. And by the way, there are guys watching your car while Jared is away this morning. So don't try to drive away now."

"Oh, wow, really? Did Jared even know about that?"

"I don't know, but Susan overheard Joseph arranging it."

"Does he have guys watching the car at night, do you think?"

"Of course not! Women are afraid of the dark!" They both laughed at that. "Anyway, I have to leave now before I get caught. Joseph should be home to check on us soon." Marina stood up and walked to the door.

Holly stood up. "Thanks for coming over, Marina.

Please be careful. I hope you don't get caught. And I hope to see you and Susan tomorrow."

"Susan also said to tell you something else. Do whatever she says at the grocery store and don't question her. People will be watching."

"All right, I'll do that. I'll follow her lead. Thank you so much, Marina. And thank Susan for me too."

Marina looked at the car parked in the driveway. "Is this your car?"

"Yeah, why?"

"How close does Jared park his truck behind it?"

"Pretty close, why?"

"How will you get out?"

Holly nodded. "You're right. Good point. I'll have to figure that one out."

Marina started walking away with Holly watching. Then she turned around with a serious expression on her face. "There's one other thing, Holly. Don't give me your answer now, but I want you to think about it. I want to go with you. I need to get out of here too." Then she turned, cut around the back of Holly's car, and disappeared in the bushes behind the shed.

Holly closed the door and sat down at the table to think about everything Marina had said. She wanted to go with her! How was that supposed to work? No, that couldn't happen. There was no way Holly could take her. There were too many consequences that could come of that.

Then Holly shook her head. Susan and Marina were

going to *help* her. How could she say no? Right now, she had to think about herself. Marina had grown up here and was used to all the craziness. Holly couldn't take a chance on something delaying her escape. Too much was at stake. Her sanity, for one.

It was all so confusing, and she didn't have anything to escape with—yet. So she would see how it all came out. And she hoped that she could go grocery shopping with them tomorrow.

Then she stood up and decided to go over every single inch of the house again to see if she could find the bullets. She'd start downstairs, put the handcuff key with her other stash, and check everywhere.

Hours later, exhausted from pushing, shoving, pulling, crawling around on the floor, and stepping up on chairs to reach spaces that she couldn't see, she looked at her watch and saw that it was almost time for Jared to get home. Holly realized that she'd better be cooking dinner when he arrived, or he might suspect something.

Opening the refrigerator, she found a pound of hamburger. Then she opened the door to the pantry and found some spaghetti and tomato sauce. She started the hamburger browning on the stove and put water to boil in the Dutch oven. Just in time, too.

Jared walked in the door and said, "Hi, honey, I'm home."

"Hi, Jared. Dinner's almost ready."

"Great, I'm starved! I had a really hard day."

"Yeah, I'll bet you did."

He sat in a chair and looked at her. "Did you have a good day today?"

"Yeah, it was fine. I'm not going to ask if *you* had a good day."

"Oh, I had a great day! Those women were all so beautiful that I didn't have any trouble—"

Holly turned around with what she hoped was fire coming out of her eyes. "I don't want to know about your other women, Jared! I don't like the idea of it! I certainly don't want to hear about it!"

He shrugged. "Well, you'll have other men soon enough."

"And I don't like *that*, either! Can we just drop it?" She put the spaghetti in the boiling water.

"Yeah, sure." He was quiet for a minute and then said, "I ran into Joseph at one of my appointments, and he noticed the boxes of wedding presents still in the truck. That's too bad, 'cause you could have worked on that today. Now you have to put them all away tonight."

Holly exhaled, turned around, and narrowed her eyes with her hands on her hips. "Now why would I have to put them all away *tonight*?"

"Because Joseph said it would be good for your discipline. He said that every time you submitted to my will, you and I would be better off for it."

"I'll tell you where you and Joseph can stick your submission and discipline." Holly turned back to the hamburger and moved it over in the pan. Then she mixed in the tomato sauce, stirred it, and stirred the spaghetti with another spoon.

"Well, I guess I can bring them in, and we don't have to tell Joseph that you didn't put them away tonight." When Holly didn't answer, he said, "I'm hungry. How soon is dinner ready?"

"Ten minutes."

"I'll be right back." Jared walked out the door leaving it ajar. When he returned, he lugged one of the big boxes of gifts and set it in the living room. Then he went back out the door and brought in another, and then did it a third time for the last box. By the time he finished, Holly had dinner on the table, so he sat down. "I love spaghetti and meat balls."

Holly slid into her own seat. "Sorry, Jared, meat sauce tonight, no meat balls."

"But I love meat balls."

"I'd be happy to make them for you right now, except I don't have any more meat left. Maybe I could go to the grocery store with Susan and Marina tomorrow."

"Yeah, that's a good idea. I love meat balls. Will you make them tomorrow night, then?"

Holly nodded. "Yeah, sure, Jared. So I can go to the grocery store?"

"I'll call first thing tomorrow morning—after I talk to Joseph to arrange it—and set up an account for you at the store."

"What do you mean 'an account'?"

"Well, you can't have any *money*. Women don't handle money. You should know that!"

"Yes, I suppose I should." She gritted her teeth and took another bite of spaghetti. There had to be a way to escape this crazy place, because if there wasn't, she didn't know how she could possibly live like this.

After dinner, she and Jared took some of the gifts out of the boxes to look at them. Holly held up the old cast-iron frying pan. "You know, Joseph really takes advantage of you. How could you possibly let him open *our* gifts first — and then take what he wanted? It's crazy! You need to start standing up to him, Jared."

"Whatever. Whenever I stand up to him, he does something to make me regret it."

"Like what?"

He stood up and put his hands on his hips. "Like make me procreate with ugly women!"

"Ah!" Holly's hands flew up in the air, and she stood up and walked out of the room. "I'm going to bed!"

Jared came in after she had gotten her nightie on, and he started to get undressed. When he finished and started pulling back the sheets to climb into bed, Holly spoke up.

"Hey, why don't you take a quick shower and wash off all the other women that you've been with. I don't particularly want them sharing our bed."

Jared sighed. "It's not *our* bed, Holly. It's *my* bed, and I allow *you* to sleep in it." He walked toward the bathroom. "I don't intend on doing this every time I procreate, but I'll do it this once." In less than five minutes, he climbed into bed and shut the light off. "You probably want to please me again tonight, but I'm too tired. Maybe tomorrow."

Holly leaned up on one elbow to look at him in the dark. "Jared, do you ever think about pleasing *me*?"

"Pleasing *you*?" He laughed. "Men don't please women, women please men!" He kept chuckling until the chuckles became snores, and he was asleep.

Holly lay back on the pillow and thought how she longed for reality where men cared about women and cared about pleasing them—in many ways. At least most men. And she prayed that reality would soon be hers again. She knew one thing for sure: she would never again take her other reality for granted; and she would never take freedom for granted again.

CHAPTER FORTY-FIVE

BEFORE DARRYL CLOSED the door and eliminated the light, Olivia got a quick glimpse at the cell area. She had been wrong—there were three cells, not two, and they were smaller than she had imagined. The cells, at least the one she was in, was six feet by eight feet. The dirty mattress, not as dirty as the one she had described for Holly, smelled like vomit and urine instead of beer and urine. She would have preferred the beer smell. Every time she sat on it, she felt like vomiting herself. There was no cot, just the smelly mattress sitting on the cold, concrete floor. And in the corner she had seen a bucket, just as she had imagined. The door had closed too quickly for her to see if there was toilet paper or not, but she was glad that she had come prepared.

Olivia thought back on her brief encounter with Carter. He hadn't even looked at her, yet even from where she stood she could see that his piercing dark eyes were hypnotic. He was in too much of a rage for her to gauge his amount of charisma, but she thought that he must have plenty to spare. Otherwise he wouldn't have so many people following him blindly like little lemmings. She remembered watching him in the video, and how surprised she was that he wasn't good looking. Wasn't good looks a requirement of these religious crazies? Maybe not, because Carter didn't have them.

Her eyes were finally adjusting to the thin stream of light coming from the window in the office door. When she looked around, it surprised her to see someone in the next cell. "Oh! I didn't know anyone else was in here!"

"Yeah, I'm here. Always here," said a tired voice. "What are you doing here?"

"I wrote a book about the cult. Oh! Pardon me for calling it a cult."

"*You're* the author?" The woman sat up and put both hands on the bars to look at Olivia. "I *heard* about you! And you're right about it being a cult. That's exactly what it is. I'm only sorry that I found out too late."

Olivia stood up and held out her hand. "I'm Olivia. Nice to meet you."

The woman stuck her arm through the bars. "I'm Mary. Really great to meet you! If I had read your book before, I never would have gotten sucked into this place, and I'd have a real life by now. Instead, here I sit on this dirty bed with no hope of escape."

"Well, if I survive long enough, my boyfriend will be coming to rescue me. But I was stupid and told him not to call the rest of the day, so he only found out about me being missing a few hours ago. By the time he gets here, it might be too late." Olivia shook her head and sat with crossed legs on the mattress.

"You're right. Carter is furious about the book from what I've heard. Rumor has it that he wants to kill you, but he wants to find the 'correct' way to do it."

"The 'correct' way, huh? That sounds ominous. I wish I hadn't been so adamant about Dean not calling! He'd be here by now." They were both silent for a few minutes, and then Olivia asked, "Why are you in here?"

"Oh!" said Mary, laying back down on her cot. "Not following the ten men during ovo rule. When I fell in love with Jordan, he assured me that I wouldn't have to do that. Of course I didn't know not doing it was contingent on getting pregnant right away." She laughed through her nose, an unamusing laugh.

"Well, I didn't get pregnant, and the first time those men came over, I was too stunned to refuse—not that I was even *allowed* to refuse, but whatever. Then I started locking myself in the bathroom, and Jordan would pay the nine men off. But one of them talked, and it got back to Carter.

"He personally came over during my next ovo—Jordan didn't even know about it until he showed up—and wouldn't take no for an answer. He brought two bullies with him—Buck was one of them—to knock down the bathroom door. Then I had the 'pleasure'"—she snickered—"of being 'entertained' by Carter for several hours that afternoon. All I can say is that it wasn't making love. Not even close. When he was through, there were nine other men, including the two bullies. I got worked over pretty good that day, not even including the sex. I had a black eye, a split lip, and bruises all over. And the following day, the same scenario with the same group of roughnecks. I couldn't walk for a week.

"After that happened, I tried everything I could do to escape, but there *is* no escape from here. I don't know what your boyfriend thinks he can do, or what you think he can do, but honestly, Olivia, the only way people escape from this place is by dying. I've already tried committing suicide three times. No luck!"

"So, do you live here all the time then?"

"It's turned out that way. Can you see the cot I'm sleeping on? It didn't used to be here. There was only a mattress on the floor like yours."

Olivia squinted her eyes and saw that Mary sat on a small single cot, with a metal headboard and footboard. "Yeah, I see it."

"Well, did you notice these?" Mary reached over her head and shook something attached to one edge of the head-board—a pair of handcuffs. "There's four pair all together, so I can't possibly escape or get out of it. And every time I'm ovo, I'm hooked up to the handcuffs, and it all starts again. Well, first they don't hook me up, and I fight them, and then they hook me up again."

"Do you ever think about just giving in and going back to your—somewhat normal—life?"

"No. *Never.* The day I stop fighting is the day my life is over."

Olivia nodded at the girl's intensity. At first Olivia thought that Mary was just like Susan in her novel, but Mary wasn't like that at all. Mary was tough. Mary was a survivor. "When Dean comes to rescue me," said Olivia, "I'm taking you with me. We'll *both* get out of here."

"Olivia, I know that you want that to happen, but honestly, rescue doesn't happen in a place like this. Only sorrow happens in a place like this. Sorrow and misery. You better get used to it."

And with those words ringing in her ears, Olivia fell asleep on the dirty mattress on the cold floor. Many hours later, a voice awakened her.

CHAPTER FORTY-SIX

Shopping

JARED HAD ALREADY left for work when Joseph put his hand on the horn and left it there until Susan was out of the truck opening the door for Holly. Susan pressed something into Holly's hand and narrowed her eyes at her while Holly got into the truck.

"You were supposed to be ready!"

"I was ready! I was standing right by the door. You saw me!" Holly said indignantly.

"Hasn't Jared taught you yet not to talk back? That's all right. You'll learn soon enough." Joseph had a smile on his face that Holly didn't like at all.

Holly sat down in the backseat, and Marina nodded to her. When Holly saw that Joseph's eyes were on the road, she glanced down at the note in her hand. It said, "Do NOT react." Curious, thought Holly.

As they drove through town, Joseph whistled tunelessly.

They drove past Joseph's house, the sheriff's office, and the church. When he was in the left turn lane with his eyes on the light, Marina slid her hand across the seat and put a plastic bag containing something unknown into Holly's hand. Holly put it into her pocket without looking, but she thought it felt suspiciously like—could she dare hope—it felt like bullets!

The town was busier and more crowded here, with many businesses lining the streets. What she had thought was the main street wasn't. This part of town looked like a *real* town instead of a sparsely populated little burg. Joseph pulled into the grocery store lot and parked. "Hurry up. I hate waiting for you."

Susan exited the car and held open the door for Holly and Marina to get out. As they walked away, Holly asked quietly, "Why can't he leave and pick us up?"

"It's not done that way," said Marina, linking arms with her. "Women must always be escorted. We're not allowed to go anywhere alone. Joseph used to walk around the aisles with us!"

Susan leaned into Holly and whispered to Marina as they approached the store, "You ready, Marina? I'm going to tell her now."

"Ready," said Marina.

"Holly, I have to tell you something and you need to try not to react badly." Susan took Holly's other arm.

"It couldn't be that bad, could it?" asked Holly.

"Worse. Simon finished his 'Messianic Privilege' and will

make it official tomorrow morning at nine o'clock."

"So?" asked Holly. "I don't understand the big deal."

"Joseph will come over to Jared's house and take you—he doesn't have to wait for ovo. He's not going to tell Jared—he knows he will get upset. He's just going to show up at the house." To delay from going into the store, Susan stopped, opened her purse, and searched through it.

"Oh, no," said Holly. She almost faltered, but Marina held her up.

"Listen, Holly, we have to go in now. Go along with whatever I do or whatever I ask you. And don't say anything that you don't want overheard or repeated. We're constantly watched in this place.

"We'll get you through this, Holly. Trust me."

"All right. Let's go."

They entered the store via the automatic doors in the back parking lot. It was a good-sized grocery store for the size of the town—nothing compared to the supermarkets that Holly was used to, but bigger than she had imagined. After she and Susan each took a basket, they started down the aisles.

"Pick up anything you need, Holly. And tell me if you can't find anything." Susan pushed her cart ahead and Holly followed.

First was a well stocked meat section, and Holly picked up a whole chicken, pork chops, and two packages of hamburger. With any luck, the hamburger that she would use tonight to fix meatballs would be the only item that she would ever use. She noticed that Marina seemed somewhat subdued, but maybe that was how she acted out in public. When they came to the dairy section, Holly picked up a gallon of milk, butter and cheese, and put them into the cart. At the juices section of the refrigerated aisle, Susan picked up a quart of lemonade and put it in her basket and then held one up for Holly.

"Is that what you were looking for? Jared likes the one with the ginger kick to it."

"Yes, that's perfect," Holly agreed.

Up and down each aisle, Holly followed Susan and Marina, picking up various items along the way. Then Susan stopped at the over-the-counter drug section and held up some antihistamines. "Didn't you say you had an allergy thing going on? This would work perfect." She put one in her own cart and handed another to Holly. "It works great for me."

Holly took it, read the label, and nodded her head. "Yes, this will work. I've used it before. Thanks." She didn't have a clue why she would need antihistamines, but she trusted Susan, so she dutifully put it into her cart.

The vegetable section was last. Susan and Marina picked out a few different vegetables, Holly picked out some broccoli and some vegetables for a salad, and then they all walked to the register. After Holly's items were rung up, she said, "Jared Tanner set up an account here. I'm his wife." She felt funny saying it, but the clerk nodded, wrote something down, bagged her groceries, and handed them to her.

As the three women walked through the automatic doors, Susan said, "You did great in there, Holly. Walk slow now, like what you're carrying is weighing you down. Put two of the antihistamines into the lemonade. The ginger will cover any trace of it. It will make him sleep. I'll do the same with Joseph tonight—because I'm hoping you'll take Marina with you—she got her period yesterday."

"Oh, no! Yes, of course I will. But—but if she does something to get me caught—"

Marina stayed silent and Susan said, "She won't. But if she gets caught somehow, she will make sure that you're not implicated in any way. Don't worry about that. What time do you think you'll leave? It should be after dark, of course, but not late enough for the antihistamines to wear off."

"I was thinking around nine-fifteen."

"That sounds perfect. Marina will be there at eight-forty-five to be safe. Good luck to you." Susan hesitated. "And don't forget about the deputy patrol at night. He sweeps the whole town with that bright light. Don't let him catch you. Either of you."

Holly forced herself not to look up with wide eyes when Susan mentioned the deputy patrol. She had forgotten about that. So she just nodded as they approached the truck. Susan put her bags in the bed of the truck, and as Holly was loading hers in the backseat with her, Susan said, "Oh, Holly. This must be yours. Joseph hates beets." And she put a paper sack with beet greens sticking out the top of it into Holly's bag.

Joseph started the truck. "I hate beets! I don't even like them in the house! Get in already, I want to get out of here."

The three women climbed into the truck with Holly wondering about the beets. On the way home as they drove past the sheriff's office again, Holly thought that if her escape didn't succeed, she would probably end up back there at Joseph's mercy. Of course if she stuck around and didn't try to leave, she'd be at Joseph's mercy anyway, just in another way.

When Joseph pulled into Jared's driveway, Susan opened the door and Holly climbed out. Before Susan closed the back door of the truck, Holly leaned down and said, "Good-bye, Marina." Then she stepped back, looked Susan in the eye, and said, "Good-bye, Susan. Thanks for taking me shopping with you." Susan nodded stoically and didn't say a word. Joseph was pulling out of the driveway before Holly had even reached the door to the house. And she hoped that would be the last time she would ever see him.

CHAPTER FORTY-SEVEN

"RISE AND SHINE! You have five minutes to get ready! Carter is waiting for you!"

"Is he talking to you or me?" asked Olivia, stretching her arms above her head.

"Both of us. You better hurry." Mary walked to the corner of her cell where her bucket was and squatted down. "I'm afraid there isn't much privacy here. Oh, do you need some toilet paper? Jordan brings it for me."

Olivia pulled out the toilet paper that she had stashed away in her pocket and held it up. "I thought that might be the case, so I took some out of the bathroom when I took the ovo test."

She had just pulled her panties up and was adjusting her skirt when a man she didn't recognize—tall, dark-haired, and dark-eyed—walked briskly into the room jingling keys. "You girls ready? Because Carter's ready for you!" He unlocked Olivia's cell and stood in front of the door barring her path. "Stick out your hands."

"What?" Olivia had no idea what he was talking about.

"Bill wants to put handcuffs on you," said Mary. "They

think that little insignificant women like us are a match for these big brutes."

"Shut up, Mary!"

Olivia put her hands out and he snapped on the handcuffs too tight. "Can you make them a little looser, please? They're cutting into my skin."

The man put his face right in front of hers and said in a high-pitched child's voice, "Do the handcuffs hurt you? Oh, isn't that just too bad!" Then he stepped over to Mary's cell and opened it.

"Bill, can't you loosen her handcuffs? She's not used to this kind of treatment. Come on, be decent for a change." She held out her hands for the handcuffs, but before he snapped them on her wrists, he slapped her across the face.

"I told you to shut up!" He grabbed her arm and shoved her toward the door. "You, too!" he said to Olivia, giving her a shove. "Follow her. She knows where to go!"

Mary used her cuffed hands to open the door, and they came outside to a brightly lit sunny day and a waiting pickup. Darryl was sitting in the front seat and the back door was open. "Hello, Darryl," Mary said as she struggled to climb in. Olivia followed her lead and used the overhead handle to pull herself in.

"Hey, Mary. Still not giving it up, huh?"

"Shut up, Darryl," Mary said, but Darryl just laughed.

Bill got into the truck, started it, and drove them toward the big, gold church. Mary looked over at Olivia. "Oh, you're real purty. Carter's going to *like* you. Too bad." She shook her head.

Olivia unconsciously stroked her hair with her handcuffed

hand. "What do you mean? I thought he was going to kill me." Olivia said it with such calm, that it surprised even her.

"Oh, he'll probably kill you all right, but it's *before* he kills you that he'll have his fun with you."

Olivia looked at her with concern. "You mean he plans to *rape* me?"

Mary nodded, but Bill said,"Shut up, Mary, or I'll hit you again. Carter doesn't *rape* anyone. He does what the Lord tells him to do. And if the Lord tells him he should *take* you, then he will. And if the Lord tells him he should *kill* you, then he will. But what he decides is none of your business, so shut up, the pair of you." Mary shrugged, and they arrived at the church a moment later.

Bill parked his truck at the back of the lot, opened his door and the back door, and Olivia followed Mary out. Then the two women, with one man in front and one behind, filed into the church, using the same entrance that Buck and Darryl had used with her the previous night. Bill marched them into Carter's office and pushed them down on an expensive looking couch that Olivia hadn't even noticed the night before. The room marked *Sanctuary* was closed.

"Sit there until Carter's ready for you. And shut up!" Bill looked at them with narrowed eyes and walked across the room to talk to Darryl.

Mary leaned over and whispered into Olivia's ear, "What time is it?"

Olivia looked at her watch. "A little after nine o'clock."

"If he doesn't come out soon, there's a chance he'll only have time to do one of us. I'll try to get him to take me first— it will at least spare you the indignity *this* time. But I may not be around *next* time."

The Sanctuary door opened, and Carter held it out so a dreamy-eyed young girl could walk out. Still buttoning her blouse, she looked at him with adoration, and he smiled warmly at her. She couldn't have been more than sixteen years old. As she walked from the room, she never took her eyes from his. He blew her a kiss as she passed through the doorway to the outside.

Mary elbowed her. "See? Not all of us think he's a lunatic."

"He just had her and he still wants us?" wondered Olivia.

"Carter is insatiable. Here he comes."

Olivia looked up to see Carter heading straight toward her with a huge smile on his face. "I didn't realize how lovely you were, my dear," Carter said as he picked up one of her cuffed hands and held it in both of his. "Before I condemn you to death, I think that we should get to know each other better. Come with me." He started to pull her up, but Mary stood up and jerked on his sleeve.

"Carter, how 'bout me first today? I'm *really* ready for you today!" Mary looked up at him adoringly. If Olivia hadn't known better, she would have believed it.

Carter stepped back and pushed her down. "I've *had* you before! You can wait!"

Mary bounced back up, wrapped one leg around one of his, and pushed her pelvis and her breasts into his body. "Oh, come *on*, Carter. *She* can wait," she said seductively.

He pushed her down again—hard—and slapped her face. "You can wait!" Anger erupted in his eyes as he glared down at her. "Leave me alone!" Then he looked at Olivia again, and his expression completely changed. He smiled at her kindly and gazed into her eyes like she was the only woman on the planet.

Olivia found herself smiling back. She couldn't get enough of how he was looking at her. Dean loved her—she had no doubt about that—but he had never looked at her like *this*. No wonder these women fall at his feet, she thought in a single moment of clarity. She tried to tear herself away and found that she couldn't and that she didn't want to. He made her feel like the whole world revolved around her—and she liked that feeling. Why should she have to give it up?

"Now let's get better acquainted, shall we?" He smiled at her again and stroked her cheek.

All Olivia could do was nod. And as he gently led her into his Sanctuary, she followed like a little lamb, looking up at him and hoping that he wouldn't look away.

CHAPTER FORTY-EIGHT

Preparation

As HOLLY OPENED the door to the house, she glanced back to see Joseph's truck disappear down the street. Good. He didn't stop at the station to see Jared. And even better —two cars were at the pumps, with one waiting. That would keep Jared busy. She hurried into the house, put the bags of groceries on the floor to save time, and glanced at the hook on the wall where she had put her keys—and they were gone. Jared had taken them away. That was all right. She hadn't locked it and wasn't going to start the car anyway; but thank goodness she had that extra key.

When she stepped back out the door, she checked to see that the cars were still at the station, and then she slipped into her car without closing the door. She didn't want to make any unnecessary noise. Releasing the hand brake slowly, she allowed the car to drift back by itself two feet down the sloped driveway. That should be enough, and any more than that might arouse Jared's suspicion. Without stepping on the brake, she pulled the hand brake and stopped the car. Reaching up to flick off the switch that controls the overhead light that comes on when the door opens, she smiled with satisfaction. Then she slipped out of the car again, trying to close the door as gently as possible —but still getting it to close all the way—and reentered the house.

After breathing a thankful sigh, she went straight for the beets. What was that about? When she put her hand in the bag, she understood. Thank you, Susan, she said to herself, and pulled out two long lengths of twine and a pair of hand-cuffs, complete with the key. She used the key to open them and then put them into her pocket. When she felt the object that Marina had given her, she grabbed it and pulled out a plastic bag with two bullets in it. And thank you, Marina!

Holly took her new treasures into the bedroom and began putting them under the mattress on her side of the bed. What if Jared suddenly decided to switch sides tonight? She couldn't take any chances, so she kept them on her side, but put them closer to the foot of the bed where she could still reach them.

Rushing downstairs to the bedroom, she moved the sailboat picture away from the wall. Remembering to start turning the combination to the left first, she opened the safe, retrieved the gun and the clip, closed the safe, turned the dial to zero, and replaced the picture on the wall, so every-thing looked exactly as it did before.

She loaded one bullet into the clip, slid the clip into place — leaving one bullet in her pocket — and then retrieved the other set of handcuffs and the spare car key from her hiding place inside the heater compartment. Forcing herself to walk upstairs slowly, she was starting to believe that her escape might really work. Because if it didn't — that possibility was just too horrible to contemplate. Between the mattress and box spring, she stuffed the gun, the handcuffs, and the key.

Holly set about putting all the groceries away, and she felt so elated at how everything was turning out, she started whistling. When she finished, she put some water on to boil for the hot chocolate she had bought at the store. Hot chocolate with marshmallows. She was living dangerously. She laughed at the irony of it all.

A few minutes later, as she sat slowly sipping the dark liquid with little marshmallow puffs floating in it, she thought about Susan and Marina. If not for them, she could be stuck here forever. Marina would definitely be going with her tonight when she left. She had no doubt that Marina would be waiting in the car when it was time to go. But, Susan — poor Susan had to stay here and put up with that abusive jerk Joseph.

No! She didn't! Holly would take Susan with her. She had to. In all good conscience, she couldn't leave another woman behind to suffer that kind of abuse. Granted that would make her escape that much more dangerous and more liable to fail, but Holly's heart wouldn't let her leave

Susan behind. She had been too kind to her. It didn't start out that way, but it certainly ended up that way. Without those two, Holly didn't know what might have become of her.

The afternoon passed way too slowly for Holly. It didn't take much time to search for the car keys in the kitchen and in Jared's bedroom. So he didn't just put them away somewhere, he definitely hid them from her. Too bad, Jared. I have other ideas for my life than being trapped in this crazy place.

She wanted the day to be over, the night to be over, the escape to be over, and she wanted to feel the cool breeze of freedom. After eating a grilled cheese sandwich for lunch, she had two more cups of hot chocolate, and despite her efforts to block out the idea, she knew that she couldn't leave without Susan. The idea may be reckless, Holly thought, but after all Susan had done for her, she had to take her. How, she didn't know.

Holly had taken antihistamines before. They weren't sleeping pills. Jared and Joseph may go to sleep, but they wouldn't be "out." She couldn't get careless thinking that they were.

Late in the afternoon, she started dinner, poured the lemonade, put in the two capsules of antihistamine, and put the glass in the refrigerator. Before long, Jared walked through the door. "Honey, I'm home!"

Jared always said it to be funny, and it was—considering that she was kidnapped, abused, handcuffed to a bed, and forced to marry Jared. And not to mention that if she stayed another day Joseph would rape her. Still, when he said it, she laughed.

"Mmmmm. I can smell the meatballs! Thanks, Holly!"

She turned around and batted her eyes at him. "You know I only want to please you, Jared!"

He smiled at her. "Maybe tonight, you'll get your chance! I'm going to wash up now."

"Jared," she called to him as he walked out of the room, "I was talking about spaghetti and meatballs!"

Holly shook her head at the comedic situation. Here she was spending the last day—the last few hours—with the man who had kidnapped her and whom she was now "married" to. Yes, she had that brief lapse of Stockholm Syndrome when she thought she was in love with him, but it didn't take long to figure that one out. Though when she thought about Jared—about how kind and gentle he could be when Joseph or Simon weren't telling him what to do— she thought that he *could* be the kind of guy she could fall for. Barring, of course, that he lived in a cult like this one. Don't go getting soft on him, she told herself.

Jared interrupted her thoughts when he returned to the kitchen and sat down. "So what did you do today?"

Holly put the glass of lemonade, a place setting, and silverware in front of him. "Went to the market with Susan and Marina. Thanks for setting up that account, by the way. It will come in handy. Then I had lunch and several cups of hot chocolate, cleaned a little," she lied about that, but oh, well. "And then started cooking dinner for my handsome husband." She hoped she wasn't going too far with that.

"Perfect!"

"How was your day?" She served him some spaghetti and put plenty of meatballs on his plate.

"Same-o, same-o. Although it seemed busier than usual. It was like everybody ran out of gas all at once." He took a bite of meatball. "Oh, Holly, this is delicious! I knew you were a keeper!"

"You betcha, big boy!" Holly sat down and started eating.

They talked about mundane topics until after Jared had his third helping of meatballs. "I'm stuffed!" He put down his fork. "Listen, Holly, I have to talk to you about something."

CHAPTER FORTY-NINE

BEFORE CARTER CLOSED the door behind them, Olivia heard Mary shout, "Oh, no! He's done it to her, too! Olivia! Fight it! Fight it, Olivia! You can do it!" But Olivia didn't want to fight it. She wanted to stay right here, safe and secure with Carter.

"Sit here, my dear." Carter showed her to a long, wide couch. She sat down on the couch, ignoring the wet spot beside her and looking up at him adoringly. He pulled something out of his pocket. "Hold out your hands, my dear, and let's get those nasty handcuffs off you." Olivia held out her hands, and he unlocked the cuffs and put them aside. "Now, why don't you lie down and get comfortable. Maybe start taking off your blouse for me so I can see those beautiful breasts of yours."

Olivia stretched out on the couch, slipping her shoes off without being asked. As she started unbuttoning her blouse, she heard someone pounding on the Sanctuary door. She ignored it. All she could think about was keeping those wonderfully dark and seductive eyes on her. Carter sat down beside her, his pants already unzipped and open.

Then the door burst open and Mary rushed in. "Olivia! Stop what you're doing! Wake up! Get out of here while you have the chance. Delay a little longer, and you'll be safe! Hurry! Get up!"

Olivia, her eyes unfocused and her head spinning, didn't understand at first what Mary was saying. But when Carter jumped up and started shouting, her head cleared. "Get out of here!" he roared. "Get out! Get out! Get out! How *dare* you disturb me when the door is closed! Darryl, Bill, come and get this young woman and hold her for me. Now!" He tried to push her out the door, but she struggled to get past him. When she noticed that Olivia had stood up and was re-buttoning her blouse, Mary nodded her head and allowed the men to pull her out the door.

Carter turned around to see a different woman awaiting him than the one he had just charmed to his couch. Olivia stood at the back of the room with a pen in one hand and her book in the other. They were the only items of "defense" that she could find in his small desk in the corner. When he started approaching her, she held them up, and at the same time tried not to look into his hypnotic eyes. "Stay away from me, Carter. Just stay away."

"Come on, my dear," he said softly. "Let's get back to where we were before we were so rudely interrupted. Come on. I'll make you feel *good*. It's the Lord's wishes that you come to me now."

"And the Lord's wishes that I die after that, Carter? I don't think so." She held the book higher and gripped the pen in her fist ready to strike down at him if he got any closer.

His manner shifted when he realized his eyes weren't

working their magic. "Do you know how many of my follow-ers are out there? All I have to do is say the word, and you're gone"—he snapped his fingers—"just like that! But I thought I'd give you a little pleasure before you are brought before the Lord."

"Give me a little pleasure." She nodded her head. "Seems like *you're* the one who gets all the pleasure here, Carter. No thank you. I don't need your kind of *pleasure*."

He took another step toward her, and when he saw her raise the book higher above her head, he thought better of it. Walking over to the couch, he stuck his hand between the end cushion and the armrest and pulled out a strong, square piece of metal, and then smiled at her as he locked it into place. Then he pulled out an identical one on the other end of the couch. "I'll have you one way or other. I *always* get what I want."

"You can attach me to your restraints if you want, but I'm not cooperating. If you expect me to lie there like a docile little lamb while you *rape* me, you better think again." Olivia remembered Mary's words about delaying before Carter had pushed her out the door. It was nearly nine-thirty now, and services began at ten o'clock.

"It's not rape if the Lord sanctions it, my dear." Carter said it calmly, as if he expected her to listen and comply.

He walked up to her and held out his hand, hoping that his gentle persona could win her over again like it did before. Olivia shuddered to think how close she had come to letting him *touch* her. It angered her to the point that she lost her composure and struck out at him with the pen, aiming for his eye. But he was quicker. He grabbed her arm and reattached the handcuffs to her right wrist. She hadn't even seen him pick them up again. Still, she wasn't about to give up. Striking out with the book as hard as she could, somehow she managed to hit him in the eye, and he faltered backwards.

"You *bitch*! You'll pay for that! You're going down *slow*. You're going down real *slow*." He made his way to the door and opened it. "Darryl, Bill, come in here and handcuff her to the couch for me."

Bill and Darryl walked into the room. Darryl came toward her, but Bill stopped at the doorway. "Carter, it's almost 9:30."

Carter turned around to look at the clock. "Oh, hell!" He zipped his pants and glared at her. "I'll still have my chance with you before we deliver your sentence. Mark my words. You're *mine*!" Then to Bill, he said, "Take her in there and handcuff her hands behind her back. Attach them to a chair somehow, and put a blindfold on her. Then take her out to the main stage." He walked back toward an easy chair and slumped down in it. "Get her out of here so I can meditate." And he closed his eyes. Abruptly, he opened them again. "You know what? I'm tired of dealing with that bitch out there, too. Handcuff her hands to a chair as well. But don't put a blindfold on her. I want her to *see* her friends and neighbors condemn her!"

CHAPTER FIFTY

Time to Go

DON'T LET IT be that he needed to lock her in the basement or anything, thought Holly. It sounded serious, but she acted as though she were merely interested. "What is it, Jared?"

"I heard a rumor today—a rumor that Simon is going to make his Messianic Privilege official tomorrow. And if he does, well, Joseph will be over here right afterward. I know him, and I know he'll do that. He probably didn't tell me so I wouldn't warn you. That would be like Joseph." Holly nodded but didn't say anything, and Jared continued. "Anyway, there's nothing you can do about it, but I thought if you knew in advance, you could—I don't know, toughen yourself up or something."

"Yeah, toughen myself up. The way that Joseph knocked me around when he arrested me and threw me in jail, it would take me ten years to toughen myself up for the

266

kind of abuse that he plans to commit tomorrow. Well, you can forget about me pleasing you tonight, Jared! I have to save myself for Joseph!" She stood up and plopped her dirty plate in the sink, breaking it.

"There's nothing else I can do or say, Holly. Sorry." He stood up and walked into the bedroom.

Holly did the dishes as slowly as she possibly could. Then she sat at the table and had two more cups of hot chocolate. She was so grateful that Susan had told her in advance about the so-called privilege. If she hadn't, Holly may have exploded much worse than she did. Of course her explosion was done deliberately to look like anger, but if she hadn't known ahead of time, it would have shocked her so much that she didn't know what she might have done.

Before too long, Holly wandered into the bedroom to see that Jared had fallen asleep with the light on. His jeans were on a chair on the other side of his nightstand, so she moved them to her side of the room, in case there was something in there that he could use to escape.

It was too early for her to leave yet, but as long as he was already asleep, she turned off the light, and climbed into bed with her clothes still on. All the sugar from the hot chocolate had given her a buzz so she wasn't sleepy. Still, if she accidentally fell asleep, the results would be worse than fatal. So she propped herself up on her elbow and stared out the window. It wasn't comfortable, but it wasn't meant to be comfortable—it was meant to keep her awake. Hours passed, and she finally spied a dim glow of moonlight coming through the window. The sliver of moon had a star so close that it looked like an earring hanging off it. It was a magical thing, and she felt it was a good omen. The moon was on its way down, and it was time for her to get up.

Was it time? Was Marina out there yet? Wouldn't she have heard something? If Marina wasn't out there, she didn't know what she would do. But Marina had promised to be ready and to be careful not to arouse any suspicion, so Holly had to trust that she'd be waiting there. Slowly, so that Jared wouldn't feel the mattress move, she crawled out of bed and retrieved her items from under the mattress.

Walking over to his side of the bed, she saw that he was sleeping on his side with one arm under his head. Perfect! She had to have the timing perfect for this. Trying not to make any noise when one side of the handcuff went around the headboard, she slipped the other side around his wrist. And then, holding each side of the handcuff in one hand, she clicked them together.

"Whaa? What's going on? Holly?" Jared moved his hand and when he found it wouldn't move, he struggled and then turned in bed so that he was lying on his back with the one wrist attached to the bed.

Holly had an inspired idea. She put the gun on the floor out of his reach and straddled his chest.

"What are you doing?"

"Something kinky, Jared. Okay? I'm really going to please you now, like no one's ever pleased you before. Trust me? Put your other hand up here now, okay?"

He was still groggy with sleep, but coming out of it fast. Still she was sitting on his chest, so he couldn't move much. Reaching behind her, she grabbed his wrist and brought it forward, moving her leg as she did so. He started struggling against her so she shifted her weight onto his free arm. With it trapped under her, she snapped the handcuff on and attached it to the headboard.

"Holly, what are you doing? This isn't funny."

Turning around and putting her weight on him again, she crawled down to the end of the bed and secured each of his feet, separately, to the footboard with the length of twine. With Jared held firmly in place, she stepped off, turned on the light, and stood above him. "I want a divorce."

"Can't we talk about this, Holly?"

"I'm leaving now, Jared." She leaned down, picked up the gun, and pointed it at him. "And if you try to follow me, I'll kill you. I swear it. You kidnapped me and now I want to leave. Don't try anything. If you really love me, you won't want to keep me here and put me through Joseph's humiliation."

Jared laughed. "I don't know how you got my gun, Holly, but there's no bullets in it! I know that for sure!"

She reached into her pocket, pulled out the second bullet, and held it out for him to see—at the same time feeling very grateful that she had the foresight to keep one bullet out to show him.

"Oh! Where did you get that?"

Although she fully intended on taking Susan with her, she still felt like she should protect her. "In the very back of your drawer." She nodded to his nightstand.

"I never had bullets in there."

Holly shrugged and flicked off the light. "That's where I found them, what can I say? Good-bye, Jared. Have a nice life."

"Come on, Holly. Take the handcuffs off. I'll let you go."

"Yeah, right, Jared. Just like you helped me escape from the jail. Good-bye." She walked into the kitchen and turned around to come back like she had just discovered that the keys were missing. "Where are the keys to my car?"

"Take off the handcuffs, and I'll tell you."

CHAPTER FIFTY-ONE

OLIVIA, SEEING CARTER sitting there with his eyes closed, thought that at least she was safe from him for now. So she didn't fight the men when they put her hands behind her back. After retrieving her shoes, they sat her down in a chair outside, next to Mary.

"How are we going to attach them to the chairs?" asked Darryl.

Bill walked to the outside door. "I've got some rope in the truck. You watch 'em. I'll be right back."

"Thank you," whispered Olivia. "You saved my life. I had no idea—"

"He's powerful, that's for sure. I'm glad you could get away from him. Although a lot of good it's going to do you in the end."

"And I'm afraid that I got you in trouble too. I'm sorry," said Olivia.

"I'm already in so much trouble, it doesn't matter. And if he kills me too, all the better."

"Shut up, you two," said Darryl, as Bill walked back in the room, carrying a rag and a length of rope cut into two pieces.

Bill attached the rope—too tight—stretching Olivia's arms painfully behind her. Then he did the same to Mary.

"Ouch! You don't have to make it that tight, you pig!" Mary screamed.

"Oh, yes I do!" said Bill, pulling the rope a little tighter.

"I'm sorry, Mary. This is my fault," said Olivia.

"Shut up or I'll stick this in your mouth to quiet you!" Bill shook the dirty rag at her, and then wrapped it around her head covering her eyes. "Come on, Darryl, let's carry 'em out to the stage."

"Why didn't we have 'em walk out before you tied 'em up?" asked Darryl.

"Shut up, Darryl, and help me. Let's do her first."

With Bill on one side and Darryl on the other, they picked up her chair and carted Olivia out—through another door that she hadn't noticed before—to the stage. Then they set her chair down. She could hear people coming into the church and sitting down, but didn't get even a hint of light from behind the dirty rag. It smelled of gasoline, and it was all Olivia could do to keep from vomiting.

"Stay here and shut up! No one here is gonna help you. And after Carter talks to them this morning, they're all going to want to kill you as much as he does." Bill gave her a small smack on the shoulder that stung, but not as much as the unflinching pain of her strained arms.

In another minute, Mary was beside her, both of them too helpless to move. "Thank you for saving me, but I think you're really in for it now."

Mary shook her head. "No big deal, Olivia. I told you—the only way out of here is dying. And now I've got that. So, in a way, you rescued me after all!" Mary was quiet for a minute and then she raised her eyebrows and nodded her head. "Listen, don't feel bad about what happened in there. I'm sure you would have come around when Carter started quoting bible verses to you."

"You mean—while he's having sex he quotes bible verses?"

"Exactly!" agreed Mary. "It's the most bizarre thing ever, and he's done it with me every single time."

The two women were quiet for a while as people shuffled into the church. Then Olivia spoke. "Mary, would you tell me what you see? I hate being blindfolded like this."

"We're sitting on a big stage with a heavy, dark-colored curtain in front of us. It will be pulled back after Carter gets out here. You can hear people coming in, right? There will be pin-drop silence out there by the time Carter arrives. They have great respect for the *charlatan*." She said the word with distaste.

"Are we alone out here?" Olivia wondered how Mary could say that in front of the two men.

"Oh, yeah. Those two big lugs left as soon as they delivered us. But Carter will be out here soon. It's nearly ten o'clock. Sometimes he likes to start early to keep people off guard. And today, he'll be eager to say his piece about you and me."

A minute later, Olivia heard footsteps on stage. She felt him tug at the rope that attached her to the chair. "Hmmm, tight isn't it? Don't worry. This pain is nothing like you'll feel *later*." Carter laughed and walked away.

Olivia stayed silent; then she heard the heavy curtains

opening. And exactly like Mary had said, there wasn't a sound coming from the audience.

There was a moment of silence, and then Olivia heard Carter say, "*I* am the Light!"

The whole congregation chanted in unison, "*You* are Thee Light."

"You are the Light," said Carter.

The congregation chanted, "We are the Light."

"*I*"—pause—"am the Messiah, and *you*"—pause—"are the power and likeness of God."

It was just like she had written in her novel. Of course, she'd gotten that from a secret camera that had been sneaked into the service at one time.

"Friends," Carter began. "Today is going to be a little different than usual. Usually, I tell you what the Lord has told me to do. But this time, in meditation, the Lord told me that I should ask *you*.

"I'm sure you've heard talk around town about a book that disparages us and belittles our way of life. How do you all feel about a book like that?"

The crowd roared angrily.

"And how do you feel about the Ungodly woman who wrote the book?"

The crowd roared again, shouting and screaming insults.

"And what should we do about a woman like that, do you think?"

"*Kill* her," screamed the crowd! "Kill her! Kill her! Kill her!" Olivia thought it sounded like they were jumping up and down.

"Shhhh," said Carter, calming the crowd. "We'll do exactly

that. And how do you think we should do that?"

"Tear her apart limb from limb!" screamed one person in the crowd, with the rest shouting agreement.

Olivia suddenly found it difficult to swallow, and her head started swimming. She tried to breathe deeply, for she feared that any second now she would faint. How could she fight back if she fainted? Feeling the strain on her shoulders, she thought, how could she fight back at all?

CHAPTER FIFTY-TWO

Freedom at Last

"Maybe the keys are in the car. I'll check out there." Holly stuck her hand in her pocket to make sure that the car key hadn't fallen out in the scuffle. It hadn't. Walking outside, she saw that the moon had already slipped past the horizon. Jared's big truck blocked the light from the gas station from illuminating her too much as she walked from the house to the car.

As she glanced around, she saw a slow-moving car with a sweeping searchlight coming straight toward her. She ducked down and hoped that he didn't see the movement. Her heart beat so fast and so hard that she thought it would burst right out of her chest. The car drove on, but she stayed put, waiting for it to turn around and come back the other direction. All she could think about was getting out of there, and now this. When it was out of sight from where she was, she crept up past Jared's truck to look down the street. The light wasn't visible, so she quietly opened the car door and stepped in. "You in here, Marina?"

"Sure am."

"Good. Stay down. The deputy with the searchlight just went by. I was just coming out the door!"

"Did he see you?"

"I really hope not. I looked and didn't see him anywhere. How far does he go?"

"All the way to the other side of town and then back again. We should go now."

"I waited a long time to get up to make sure he was all the way gone. I'd rather wait until he comes round again." As eager as Holly was to get out of there—before Jared could get loose or Joseph wake up—she thought it was foolhardy to try to beat the deputy after she had already delayed. What if he drove by as she was backing the car down the driveway? No, they had to wait.

"Holly? Susan told me about them draining the gas out of your car. Did you check to make sure they didn't do that again?"

Holly's heart felt like it fell into her stomach, and her throat got tight. "No, I never even considered that. Keep your fingers crossed." She turned the key, not enough to start the car, but enough to see the gas gauge. If worse came to worst, she would steal Jared's truck. But the gas gauge still showed full, so Holly breathed an audible sigh. "Still full. Listen, I want to go get Susan. I can't leave her here with that monster Joseph."

"Here take this." Marina reached over the seat to hand Holly a piece of folded up paper.

"I don't want to turn on the light right now. What does it say?"

"Let's get going, and I'll tell you. Don't turn your lights on right away until you're down the street a bit."

"I'm waiting until the deputy drives by again."

"But—but if Joseph wakes up and discovers I'm gone —"

"Marina, I think there's less chance of that than the deputy driving by while we're backing down the driveway. It shouldn't be much longer." Ten tense minutes later, the car and searchlight swept the area again. This time, Holly had ducked down in the seat when she saw the light approaching. "All right, let's wait until he turns around and goes back the other way. He's been gone ten minutes—that should give us plenty of time to get away."

"It usually doesn't take that long, so be careful. Be careful—but hurry."

Holly was hunkered down in the seat far enough not to be seen but upright enough to see the side-view mirror. She saw the light coming and waited for it to pass. And waited. And waited. It didn't pass, it just stayed still. But it wasn't shining on their side of the street. "Marina! Something's wrong! The light is stationary where I can see it in the mirror!" Holly whispered as if the car could hear her.

"Do you think he saw us?" Marina whispered back.

"I don't know. I'm going to slowly sit up higher so I can

see more."

"Be careful! Maybe he stopped for something else."

Holly moved slowly to get a better look at the mirror. What she saw chilled her. The car was stopped in front of the gas station, and the driver had his cell phone to his ear and a cigarette in the other hand. She could see the lit tip of the cigarette even from here. "He's smoking and on the cell phone, Marina! Do you think he's calling Joseph for back-up?"

"If he's smoking, I think it means he's not concerned. Besides, Joseph doesn't allow his deputies to smoke while on duty. He'd get in trouble. I think he's just taking a break. We have to wait and hope that Jared doesn't get loose and Joseph doesn't wake up and find me missing."

Holly kept watching, her heart beating madly in her chest. Finally, the man put the cell phone away, dropped the cigarette on the ground, and drove off, his light shining on the opposite side of the street. "He's gone, let's wait another minute or two."

"No! Let's go now! He's gone! Let's go before he gets back! Now! Come on, Holly! We need to get out of here!" Marina's voice sounded agitated.

Holly didn't know how long it would take Jared to get out of his bonds or even if he had to wait until Joseph found him in the morning, but Marina was right. They needed to get out of there. She clicked on her seatbelt thinking that being in a car accident was the least of her worries right now. The car started smoothly, and after pulling forward to avoid Jared's truck, she turned the wheel sharply and used the hand brake to let the car slide into the street. There were no cars coming in either direction and no cars parked on the street. Although she couldn't see very well, she drove for several blocks before switching on the lights.

"Do you see the deputy?" Marina sat up a little from the back.

"I don't see him, and we're almost a mile out of town. Do you want to crawl up here with me?"

"Yeah, I'll try." Marina managed to squeeze between the seats and slide into the passenger seat.

"Put your seatbelt on."

Marina clicked it into place. "Want me to read you Susan's letter?"

"I don't want to turn on the interior light and draw attention to ourselves."

"That's okay. I'll bend over and use my little flashlight. No one will see."

"All right, but be ready to turn it off if I see anything." Holly looked around and there was just darkness ahead of her and behind her. "And if I see the light coming up behind us, I'm going to floor it. So hang on if that happens!"

Marina leaned down, put her skirt up over her, unfolded the note, and turned the flashlight on. She was right. Holly could barely see any light coming from her direction.

"Dear Holly, I'm writing this note because I thought that you'd want to take me with you. You can't. If you did, Joseph would have it in for you even more than he already does and he'd never quit search-

ing. As far as you taking Marina, that would only make Joseph happy. Of course, he doesn't know yet that she had gotten her period!" Marina stopped reading long enough to laugh, then continued. *"But don't worry. Your time here has had an impact on me. I won't be staying, but I will have to leave in my own way in my own time. I can put up with Joseph's abuse and the 'gang banging' for a while longer. Then—I'm out of here. Please stay safe and take good care of Marina. And thank you for everything. Susan."*

As Marina finished reading, Holly found the onramp to the freeway and turned onto it. "I wasn't going to leave without her."

"Susan knew that. That's why she wrote the letter." Marina had already turned off the light and sat up. She put her hand on Holly's arm. "Thank you so much for getting me out of there. I know I have a lot to learn about the real world."

Holly nodded and stayed silent for a minute as she saw the distant lights of Amarillo getting brighter. She would have preferred to drive home, but Becky's home was closer; and right now she needed to feel safe and loved as soon as she could. Turning to Marina, she said, "I think you're going to like the real world, Marina. I think you're going to like it a lot."

CHAPTER FIFTY-THREE

DEAN HAD HIS team in position first, so he stood by the stage door without opening it. Cole Branson and John Hauser stood beside him. Carlos, heading the other team, would come in through the front doors. Dean's team would go immediately to the stage, where Carter was. Dean had arranged it that way because he didn't want anyone to accidentally kill Carter before he found out where Olivia was.

If Carter had already had her killed, Dean planned to tear him apart piece by piece. But not before covering him with honey and staking him out on an anthill—or something worse. Carlos had told him that he knew of just the place. He knew that John Hauser felt the same way, so Dean would have help. But he hoped that it wouldn't come to that. And he also hoped that John Hauser could find his daughter among all these disciples. If she didn't want to leave, though—well, that was another story.

His phone vibrated in his hand. He looked at the text message. "Ready when you are."

Glancing up from the phone, he whispered to the two men beside him, "You guys ready?" Each man, with a pistol in his hand, nodded. Dean tapped onto the phone "3 2 1 go!" Then he pressed the button, motioned to the men in front of him, opened the door, and the three of them rushed out on stage.

The brightness of the stage surprised him; he hadn't expected that. Carter stood in the middle with a huge sky-light above him, highlighting the white robe that he wore. But off to the side of him sat two women tied to chairs. One of them was Olivia! Dean saw that Carlos and the other team were already in place—although Dean's eyes weren't adjusted yet, he could hear the outrage of the audience.

"What do you mean by this?" shouted Carter.

Dean knew that Cole and John would take care of Carter, so he ran immediately to Olivia's side, pulled the blindfold off her face and his knife out of its sheath, and cut her loose. Realizing that John Hauser was next to him, he handed him the knife.

"It's my daughter, Dean! My daughter! Mary, are you okay?"

Then a shot rang out and Carter fell to the floor. Dean looked out at the audience to see where David Alexander was. If anyone had shot Carter, it would be him. David was at the side of the stage closest to where Dean was, and he saw David shrugging his shoulders. Then Dean saw Carlos holding onto someone's arm. Carlos had already taken the gun away from him, and the man was trying to break free.

The crowd was in an uproar, and they surrounded Carlos and tried to get at the struggling man. Carlos lost his grip, and the man managed to get away from the crowd and flee up the side steps leading to the stage. A single shot crackled through the air, the man fell, and the crowd quieted. Dean looked up to see David Alexander nodding to him, his rifle still in position.

Cole was kneeling over Carter, his fingers pressed against his neck. "He's gone, Dean."

"Check his pockets for a key, will ya, Cole?" Dean asked, helping Olivia to her feet. He could feel how weak she felt in his arms, and he held her up.

"Right here, Dean." Cole fished the key out of Carter's pocket and handed it to Dean.

"Thanks, man." He unlocked the handcuffs and then tossed the key to John Hauser so he could unlock his daughter.

Olivia struggled to her feet with Dean's help. "Oh, Dean, thank you! I'm so sorry I didn't believe you when you told me the risks! I'm so sorry!"

"Shhhh. It's okay, it's okay. You're safe now. I'll take care of you." Dean stroked her hair to calm her.

Olivia pressed up against him, but her arms were still in a semi-backward position. "And I'm sorry I can't hug you, but I can't seem to get my arms forward yet. They still hurt too much!"

"It's okay, baby, it's okay." Dean continued to stroke her hair and whisper "Shhh" into her ear. "You're safe now."

John Hauser came up beside him with his arms around his daughter. "I can't thank you enough for this, Dean. You've saved my daughter, too. Thank you!"

"I appreciate your help with this, John. You were here right beside me."

"Olivia!" said a woman's voice. "Olivia, you were right!

Your boyfriend rescued us! Thank you so much!"

"Thank you for protecting me, Mary. If it hadn't been for you—" Olivia shook her head.

"Just remember, Olivia, it wasn't your fault," said Mary. "He has that effect on *everyone*. He's hypnotic! It wasn't a failing in you, so don't blame yourself!"

"What does she mean?" asked Dean.

Olivia slowly shook her head. "I'll tell you on the way home. It's a long story."

Dean saw that Carlos and his team were ushering all the people out of the church. Cole, still standing over Carter's body, looked at him. "What do we do with *him*?" Then Cole glanced over to where the other man lay on the steps. "And *him*?"

"Leave them be. Someone will take care of them."

"Olivia, you know who that was over there on the steps?" Mary asked.

"No, I didn't see him."

"It was Buck. He said he was going to kill Carter, and he did! And now he—bully that he was—is dead, too."

"I couldn't have written a better ending myself," said Olivia. She turned to Dean. "Let's go home, Dean. We have a wedding to plan!"

"Really?" asked Dean, a big smile spreading across his face. "You sure?"

"Positive!" said Olivia, linking her now relaxed arm through Dean's. "And then I have to begin writing the nonfiction sequel to my first self-published book!"

"Oh, no!" gasped Dean, holding a hand to his forehead.

www.ingramcontent.com/pod-product-compliance
Lightning Source LLC
Chambersburg PA
CBHW061545170626
46811CB00001B/95